The Substitute Teacher: Baptism of Fire
by
Benjamin R. Robinson Jr.

I thank my Lord and Savior Jesus Christ for giving me the ability to write this book. I also acknowledge Kat, Faith, Stephen, Christian, Debbie, Reggie, those I came up with on 19th street and 21st street, substitute teachers, teachers, administrators and public school students everywhere who inspired me to write this book.

This is a work of fiction. All characters and events portrayed in this book are fictional. Any resemblance to real people or incidents is completely coincidental.

Copyright © 2009 by Benjamin R. Robinson Jr.

The Substitute Teacher: Baptism of Fire
by Benjamin R. Robinson Jr.

Printed in the United States of America

ISBN 978-0-557-11976-9

All rights reserved. No part of this book may be reproduced in any Form without the permission of the author.

Biblical paraphrasing and quotes are taken from the King James Authorized Version, 1611. All rights reserved. Contents and/or cover may not be reproduced in whole or part in any form without consent of the authors.

http://stores.lulu.com/ben_r_robinson
http://www.systemexpert.biz
http://systemxp.cloud.prohosting.com/Classwork/Project/index.html

Table of Contents

1. The Bet Is On 2
2. Baptism of Fire 10
3. Into The Blackboard Cauldron 14
4. Back To The New Grind 26
5. Assignment No. 17 28
6. The Last Straw 34
7. Pawn to King Rook Four 42
8. Day Two, Spinley Junior High School 49
9. The Thin Red Line 60
10. Song of the Substitute Teacher 70
11. Twilight Zone 72
12. Ode to King Rose 82
13. Teacher Strike 84
14. Day Two, Rosemont Elem. School 88
15. Day One, Horrible Hammond 92
16. Day Two, Horrible Hammond 102
17. School Daze 106
18. Where's Karen? 117
19. Counter Attack 123
20. Showdown With Matson 129
21. Letter of Gratitude 137

1. The Bet Is On

Graduating from college and returning to Democracy City to find a stock clerk job wasn't my idea of success. What had I gone to school for? To sweep some floors? I guess I had to start somewhere. Was it all my fault? Or was I just a sacrificial pawn on a gigantic chess board in the process of being eliminated from the employment game? My liberal arts degree didn't seem to carry enough weight in the job market. I had been on a thousand interviews to no avail. They said I was either 'over qualified' or 'under qualified'.

This was me, C. J. of D.C., Democracy City, not Moe Joe. It seemed as if I was just another number on an application in a pile of others waiting to be rejected.

Why me? I asked myself, why was I having such a hard time? Was I a failure or something? Was I being punished for the wrong I had done in the past? I tried to treat people right and do the right thing most of the time. We had corporal punishment back in the day but I was always a good student and never gave the teacher any problem. In school we said the Lord's prayer and flag salute every morning. We had the ten commandments on the bulletin board. My mother used to send my brother and me to Sunday school. When I got out of high school, I stopped attending Sunday school. I thought that since my mother didn't come with us, then why should I continue to go?

I wasn't an atheist, I just wasn't sure if there was a God or not. My mother had always told us "God don't like ugly and ain't crazy about beauty," and "that there was a God somewhere."

I still wasn't convinced. If God existed, then why did he allow so many bad things to happen? I didn't want to take any chances. So just in case God did exist, I was going to try to keep some of the commandments. I knew I couldn't keep them all, but if I kept some, maybe God would let me in to heaven, if there was a heaven. Two good things, Watergate was over and the Vietnam war had ended and I didn't have to go. My father had served in the army in the Pacific during World War Two. If I had been drafted, I would have gone, to continue the tradition. I had taken two years of ROTC and I could have gone on to Officers' Candidate School and become a ninety day wonder. I was glad that I had been granted a college deferment. I decided not to go to Officers' Candidate School.

My mother and father had encouraged me to go to college and get my degree. That seemed to be my prime directive in life. Now that I had it, I was getting frustrated because it seemed as if I couldn't do anything with it.

I got off the bus and barely missed colliding with some religious fanatics holding signs saying 'Jesus Saves'. I wondered what made people walk up and down the street carrying signs like that.

The Board of Education building loomed up before me. I slipped through the revolving doors and entered the elevator and pressed seven. That was a lucky number, I hoped. I walked out of the elevator and nervously down the hall toward the Examiner's office. I stepped into a spacious office as I wiped perspiration from my forehead. Behind the desk was a middle aged man in an expensive gray pin-striped suit. He looked at me with satisfaction and relief.

"Well Mr. Johnson, we've chosen you for the substitute teaching position, congratulations."

At last I could use my degree. But the last thing I wanted to do was teach. I've always wanted to be somebody, to make a difference in the world. Not be like the guys who just hung on the corner. I wanted to discover a cure for cancer, rocket to the moon, build a time machine. I used to read a lot of science fiction. I wanted to do something great. Teaching hadn't been on my agenda but I had to do something to make ends meet.

After riding the bus home, I marched up the street like an elite guardsman on parade. I was careful to avoid the empty wine bottles and assorted debris that littered the sidewalk. My father had tried to warn me about moving into the Stevenson Pride Apartment complex, but I wouldn't listen.

I should have known something was wrong. On the first day I moved in, the people across the hall were fighting in the hallway. But it would be only temporary. I told myself, until I could find something better. I entered my apartment. Karen greeted me with a hug and kiss. Karen and I first met on a blind date. She was a man's dream come true. She had a figure like the cartoon character 'Betty Boop', sunshine in her smile, and her light brown skin was smooth as silk. And she loved to make love. No matter how many times I was out of work, she never put me down, but always encouraged me. What more could a man ask for in a woman?

Karen loved me and had asked me several times to marry her. But I just couldn't do it. I had bad memories of how my mother and father used to fight before they divorced. And after that, I told myself I would never get married. Why get married anyway when I could just live together with

Karen? I wondered why they called it 'living in sin?' It didn't seem to be such a bad thing to me.

"How'd it go? Did you get the job?" Karen asked.

"Of course I got the job, a substitute teaching job," I boasted.

"I'm so glad, Cornell," Karen was relieved.

"I need a drink to celebrate," I chuckled.

"There's none left, you have to go and get some more," Karen suggested.

"I guess I will."

"Don't get tied up with those guys on the corner," Karen cautioned.

"I won't, I'm coming straight back." I promised.

On the way to the store, I ran into some of the boys, Matson, Confused, and Leroy, and did exactly what I told Karen I wouldn't do.

"What's hap'nin dude?" Matson yelled as he stood defiantly in his black leather pants and black silk body shirt. His bald head glistening in the sunlight. Matson inevitably had attained the level of my neighborhood nemesis. When we were coming up together we used to fight each other every other day, over trivial things like who would be first up at bat. And now it seemed that every time I tried to get on the fast track, he was there bugging over my shoulder, signifying to me that I was still a lame and not slick enough to make it.

"You got it," I said as I gave him the old hand shake.

"What's been going on with you?" Confused asked superficially. Confused had a lot of sense until he would start drinking some wine, then he would get confused about things.

"I just landed myself a new job."

"Oh yeah? What kind of job slick?" Leroy asked sarcastically as he pulled out a bottle of King Rose wine and offered me some.

"A substitute teacher job," I replied. I took the bottle and almost tried to drink the whole thing.

"Why are you teaching, the big money's in private industry." Leroy asserted.

"I'm doing this to hold me over until I find something else."

"How's Karen?" Confused asked sincerely.

"She's doing fine, just fine." I wished he wouldn't ask about her. I didn't want anyone messing with my Karen.

"Why did you go to school Cornell? I know you're smart but I can't see spending four years in school just to teach." Matson croaked.

"I didn't go to school to be a teacher. I hate teachers and I hate school. I went to school to get away from home, to avoid the draft, and to get a good job." I began to feel uneasy at Matson's probing questions.

"Ain't no money in teaching. Why don't you get out here with us and make some real money, sell some dope, be a hustler, run some numbers, pimp, strong arm, bootleg, do something. You ain't gonna' ever make any real money by working for it. Work all your life, then retire with a few bucks a month pension and gold watch. You don't want that do you?"

By now my head was spinning slightly from the wine. I struggled to sustain my composure.

"No Matson, I'm going to make my money straight. Why take all of those chances hustling?" I tried to convince Matson, but I knew it was in vain. Matson only knew the way of the street. He looked down on anyone who tried to play by society's rules.

Matson paused for a moment and took another swig from the bottle of 'King Rose' wine. The wine seemed to have no effect on him while it was causing me to feel a little light headed. "That might be your opinion Cornell, but you gotta face the facts, you're just another nigga out here trying to survive the system just like us."

The 'King Rose' wine gave me a false sense of confidence so much to the point that I said a very foolish thing.

"I tell you what Matson, I bet in a year, starting today, September seventh to this time next year, with me just using my head to make money legally, I'll have more than you will by hustling." What was I saying, I asked myself, curse that 'King Rose' wine.

"You got yourself a bet Cornell, you got yourself a bet. And I'll bet you a thousand dollars I'll have more than you within a year," Matson said with a broad smile on his face.

"That's a bet," I said as we shook hands on it. "I think I'm going to cut out Matson, I'll be checking with you off and on. I started walking away.

"Cornell," Matson's voice boomed to me as I reached the next corner.

"Yeah." I turned around.

"I don't want to have to come looking for you for my money at the end of the year. You know I don't play when it comes to my money."

"I don't want to have to come looking for you either Matson," I said trying to sound as bad as Matson. Who was I fooling?

I walked back home wondering what I had done. But I couldn't let Matson make a fool out of me. After all, I had gone to college, I wasn't stupid. And besides, at the rate Matson was going, I figured he'd be either in jail or dead in a year anyway. I wondered if I would have the courage to go after Matson if he didn't want to pay. I sobered up fast when I realized that it would be mandatory that I did. If word got out that Matson owed me that much money and I didn't make an effort to collect, I wouldn't even be able to show my face on the street again. And how would I be able to collect from him? I knew Matson had two or three guns and I didn't have any. I might have to buy one sooner or later. I knew if I lost the bet, Matson would track me down.

After I told Karen what had went down, she became hysterical.

"Why did you make a stupid bet with Matson?! Everyone knows

he's selling dope and has some girls working on the corner." Karen was angry with me.

"How are you going to make more money than him by just working? And you know he will come after you for the money if you loose the bet. Whether you two are friends or not, you know the law of the streets. If someone owes money, they have to pay up or else. I love you Cornell and I just don't want to see anything happen to you over some stupid bet!" Karen was sobbing in tears.

"Don't worry Kay," I pulled her into my arms hugging and kissing her gently, "at the rate Matson is going, he'll be dead or in jail before the end of the year." I tried to sound confident, but it wasn't working. I wanted to tell Karen I loved her, but I just couldn't bring myself to do it. What was wrong with me? Why couldn't I tell her? I think I did love her. The guys I grew up with had said never fall in love. That I could lie and tell a woman I loved her, but never really mean it. I had the opposite problem. I would fall in love with every woman I met, but I couldn't bring myself to tell them I loved them.

By now I didn't want anything to drink so I put the King Rose wine in the refrigerator. Karen prepared a delicious meal of fried chicken, mashed potatoes and collard greens. That's another thing Karen could do well, was cook. And boy, could she cook, in the kitchen and in the bedroom.

After watching the news and some late night TV, Karen put on the 'Delphonics' and 'Barry White'. We snuggled up together and had a romantic interlude before falling asleep.

My sleep was interrupted as I bolted up in bed in a cold sweat. The last thing I remembered seeing was Matson's bald head laughing at me in my dream.

"C. J. what's wrong?" Karen inquired as she held me tightly.

"Nothing, I just had a bad dream, that's all."

"Here, come closer." Karen whispered sweetly, "I got something for you that will take all of your bad dreams away."

We had another romantic interlude and this time I drifted off into a sweet sleep.

2. Baptism of Fire

I had my strategy all mapped out. The bet was on. I knew I had to win this. If I didn't, I knew Matson would be after me and have to carry out the street primary directive. Whoever didn't have the money if they lost would be blown away, despite the friendship we had while we were growing up. Matson would not be able to afford to show me any mercy and still maintain his credibility as a hustler on the streets. It was the law of the 'street jungle'. What had I gotten myself into?

I put my eyeglasses on, slipped into my bargain-basement suit and gulped down my breakfast, scotch and grape juice. I was really jittery. I was always a little shaky when I started on a new job. I swallowed one of Karen's tranquilizers. Just in case. I caught the bus to Kilmer Junior High School.

"I'm a substitute reporting for my assignment." I said like an untried soldier replacement on his first mission.

"Your name?" The secretary asked, her eyes on me intently.

"Cornell Johnson."

"Sign in here."

I signed my name.

"Here's the key for room 207. If you have any problems, just send a student down to the office."

"All right." I took the key and walked up the steps to the second floor. Kilmer Jr. High hadn't changed since I had been a student. The hallways, the rooms, ceilings and graffiti on the wall looked the same. I walked into room 207, flipped the light on and hung my coat up. I wondered how the day would go. I sat behind the desk and checked the regular teacher's schedule. Gillmore: homeroom 7-5, period I 8-4A, Algebra I, period II 8-1, Algebra. I, period III -free period, period IV, 7 -6B, General Math, period V, 9-2, . Algebra II, period VI-lunch, period VII-duty.

I looked in the teacher's desk for assignments and found one as my students came in. By 9:15 I finished checking the roll and reading the morning announcements from the daily bulletin. My homeroom ended and my first period class started. I passed out the dittoed assignment. The students worked quietly and I only had an occasional problem. Before I knew it, the period was over and the students passed in their work. My second period class was uneventful except for a few pieces of paper that were tossed across the room. The bell rang indicating the end of the second period and the beginning of the third, my free period. I didn't have anything else to do so I thumbed through the Substitute Teachers' Manual and turned to the section on classroom discipline, which outlawed corporal punishment.

The fourth period began and I thought that the rest of the day would be easy. The tranquilizer in my system further reinforced the idea in my sluggish mind. The fourth period class entered the classroom more noisy than the previous ones. This was a sign of things to come.

Before I knew it the kids started to scream and yell at each other. I turned to my right and just barely avoided being hit in the head with an eraser. As if this was a signal, objects of all sizes and shapes began to fly back and forth across the classroom.

"Sit down boy, what's wrong with you!" I screamed, to no avail as one student had gotten hold of a bucket full of water and proceeded to splash the other students, blackboard and floor. I was startled as a student threw a chair across the floor, attempting to hit another student.

By this time I had lost all control of the classroom as students ran in and out of the classroom at will, totally ignoring my pleas for order. I arose to my feet and made one last vain effort to restore order.

"Stay in or out of the classroom!" I yelled at a student who had been running in and out of the classroom jubilantly, as if he were at some kind of carnival or something.

"What are you going to do if I don't listen to you, hit me?"

For a split second I was about to hit him, but I regained my composure, remembering section five, under classroom discipline, 'no corporal punishment allowed.'

I finally had enough and walked out and down to the office. By now I was shaking and my nerves were unraveling. I was too embarrassed to admit to the assistant principal that I had lost control of my classroom.

"I have to leave," I told the assistant principal, "there's been an emergency at my home," I finished as I walked out of the school in relief. I told myself I would definitely have to find myself another job.

3. Into The Blackboard Cauldron

I reconsidered the situation and decided not to quit just yet. This was me, C. J. of D.C., Democracy City. Was I going to let those kids run me away? I told myself I could handle them. It was just that on my first day I didn't now what to expect. In any event I didn't think I had a choice but to continue to substitute for the time being. With theoretically less dangers to face than Matson, I hoped I would be able to outlast him.

Bangley was an old school. What I didn't know was that the principal was retiring and discipline was slack, no doubt the principal didn't' t want to press his luck by being too hard in his last year. The result, the students were having a field day, especially with substitutes.

My homeroom students began to trickle in. "Good morning, my name is Mr. Johnson, I'm your substitute for today," I continued as I read the daily bulletin. Some students were' still chatting as I read it.

"Could you quiet down, while I call the roll please," I said. The students quieted down a little.

"Tina Marshall."

"Here."

"Felicia Johnson."

No answer.

"Felicia Johnson," I repeated, "is Felicia Johnson here."

"No," a student said, "she got suspended."

"Oh o.k." I continued.

"Daren Stasher."

"Yassuh." The class burst into laughter.

"Just say here or present please," I said.

"Stephanie Harris."

"Here," a boy answered, and the class started laughing again.

"Is that your name boy?" I asked.

"No, Miss Johnson, I mean Mr. Johnson," another student giggled.

"Stephanie's not here today."

"Warren Ford."

No answer.

"Is Warren Ford here?" I asked impatiently.

"He's here," a girl said, "Warren, why don't you answer to your name?"

"Is Warren here? Where's Warren?" I asked again.

The students pointed toward a boy with faded jeans on and a stocking cap on his head. I looked at him and he gave me a mean look.

"Are you Warren?"

"Yeah, I'm Warren"

"Why don't you answer to your name then?"

"Do you believe in God?" Warren asked me. This question took me completely by surprise. All of a sudden, the question triggered a cascade of memories. Momma used to tell me and my brother, "there's someone greater than man." I almost became a believer while listening to the radio one afternoon. I heard the preacher say "…just put your hands on the radio and feel the power of God…" I decided to do what he suggested, saying all along that I wouldn't feel a thing. To my surprise, I did feel something. But I told myself, it must have been my imagination. I couldn't have felt anything. I only thought I had.

"I don't know if He exists or not." I finally responded.

"Do you believe in demons?" Warren asked me another crazy question.

"If I don't know if God exists, then why should I believe in demons?" I snapped back.

"Well, I'm going to send one tonight to kill you."

"Ha ha, that's funny." Now I really started to chuckle. I didn't know if God existed let alone demons. And besides, why would a demon, if it did exist, do what the boy wanted him to do anyway. I dismissed the thought and continued calling the roll.

"Lolita Cooke."

"Here."

"Yvette Thornton."

"Here."

I called out fifteen more names. The first period began as the other students passed out of the room. Nervously I reached in my pocket and downed a tranquilizer. The day had barely started and already the students were getting to me. But I was determined to maintain my composure.

The students outside in the hallways were making as much noise as they possibly could, some were running, pushing, shouting and cursing at each other. I stood outside the door at my duty post.

"Where's Mrs. Kimberly?" a student asked.

"She's not here today, I'm the substitute."

"We got a sub!" the student yelled to the others with glee, passing the word, "We got a sub! We got a sub!"

I stepped back into the room. Students came in making as much noise as they could. The teacher didn't leave an assignment so I would have to play it by ear. After the students took their seats I introduced myself again.

"Mrs. Kimberly didn't leave you any work today so you can have a free period." I sat down behind her cluttered desk. I later would realize that giving them a free period was a mistake..

"Are you married, Mr. Johnson?" One girl asked looking at me intently.

"No."

"Do you have a girl friend? Another student asked.

"Yeah, but..." the questions from the students were taking me by surprise.

"Are you a teacher?" another student asked.

"No, I'm just a substitute."

"What school did you go to?"

"I went to the University of . . . "

"Stop asking Mr. Johnson all those questions." One student spoke out.

"That's all right, I don't mind answering some of your questions." I was starting to get used to the craziness.

"Are you from here?"

"Yes, I'm from here, D.C. Any more questions?"

"Can you defend yourself, Mr. Johnson?" another student asked.

"Yes, I can, why?"

"This school is rough. Mr. Johnson, you better be careful."

Before long the period was over. I contemplated for a moment what the student had said and took another tranquilizer just to be on the safe side. I asked myself what kind of school was this? Before the day was over, I would find out.

Before I could get up out of my seat, two students came in cursing at each other.

"Your mother." a short fat little boy in green pants and a red and white striped T-shirt yelled.

"I know you're not talking about my mother Jimmy, because I'll knock your head off!"

"Try it if you..."

Before I could break them up the two students were swinging away at each other with a flurry of punches.

"Break it up!" I screamed as I separated them.

"You two break it up now and sit down like you have some sense." After I broke up the fight, the two students sat down and glared at each other. The rest of my second period entered and took their seats. I took attendance and told the students the teacher didn't leave an assignment. When I said that, the students cheered.

As I looked across the room, a student threw a pencil at another student's head. As if this was a signal for the rest of the class to throw pencils, pieces of paper, paper clips and anything else at each other. Pandemonium ensued. Here we go again. As soon as I got one group to stop, another group of students would start throwing things.

"You people are going to have to stop throwing things at each other!" I yelled angrily. I was getting disgusted. Then suddenly the class stopped throwing things and became silent. I wondered what was going' on now. Then I turned toward the door and saw the figure of a short , well-dressed gray-haired man in a gray business suit staring into the classroom.

"Good morning, I'm Mr. Caldwell the principal. Is this class giving you any trouble?"

"Yes they are," I said with relief. "They're throwing things at each other."

"I want you people to give this man some respect! Now act like you have some sense!" He said sternly. "If you have anymore trouble out of this class, let me know, Mr., Mr..."

"Johnson," I said.

"Mr. Johnson, just let me know, and I'll take care of them." He said as he left.

The bell crackled and I was thankful the second period was over. By now I felt sluggish. I was glad the next period was my free period. I decided to try to stay on my feet so I wouldn't fall asleep from the effect of the tranquilizers.

How did the other teachers make it? I locked the classroom door and asked the teacher next door where the teachers' lounge was. I walked into the teachers' lounge and observed a policeman talking to two female teachers. One of the teachers was very attractive. I contemplated asking her for her phone number. Then I thought about it and decided not too. If Karen found out I was trying to see another woman behind her back, she always told me she would kill me and the other woman.

"I don't know what to do officer Simms. Some of these students come to class high off of dope or drunk or smoking that stuff. Their parents don't care, the parents are probably doing the same thing. How can I teach them anything." I heard one teacher say to the officer as I sat down.

"Just tell me who they are, I'll take care of them. Put them in a detention center, They'll straighten up. The officer boasted.

"Good morning, are you a substitute?" One speckle-faced teacher asked.

"Yes, I am," I said as I sat down.

"Who are you in for?"

"Kimberly."

"Kimberly? She's got some bad classes. I hope you can handle them. I had a boy from her homeroom the other day I had to send down to the office to get suspended."

"They're giving me a little trouble, but I think I can handle them."

Who was I fooling?

"I hope so."

I sat back and lit up a cigarette and the officer started looking at me strangely.

It dawned on me that he might be wondering what I was on. The tranquilizers were probably making my eyes look funny. I turned away from him and tried to ignore him, but I could feel his eyes penetrating my back. He finally turned away and continued talking to the teachers. I thought to myself this cop wants to bust everybody, and probably even me if he had the chance.

"They really beat Jerry up the other day in the cafeteria, did you hear about it, Mrs. Saxon?" The other teacher asked while she crossed her legs in a sexy manner.

"Yes, I did. Wasn't it because the kids thought he was snitch or something?"

Mrs. Saxon continued, "Officer Simms, was it true? Was Jerry an informant?"

"I don't know anything about that." Officer Simms answered, not wanting to expose Jerry as an informant.

"I finished my cigarette and was fighting off sleep. The bell DINGDONGED and I got up and went back to my classroom. Fourth period.

The kids came in and sat down. This time I thought I'd just pass out a piece of paper and let the students sign their name on it. Calling out the roll seemed to be too time consuming. As I sat back trying to recuperate from the first two periods, I overheard a few students talking about the incident in the cafeteria. "Did you hear anything about it Mr. Johnson?" A well-dressed eighth grade student asked me.

"No, I don't know anything about it."

"You're not undercover are you?" another student questioned.

"No, I'm not." That question really got to me. Did I look like I was undercover?

"I hope you're not. You see what happened to the last snitch, we got him good in the cafeteria.. "

"Now wait a minute now. I told you I'm not working undercover. Are you threatening me or something?"

"No." the student backed off.

"Leave that man alone Cheryl, he's no undercover, can't you tell? He's just a substitute." A tall round-faced boy said.

"You know," Cheryl said to the boy, "I like him. He's cool."

The tall, round-faced boy snickered. I kept myself from blushing. I was cool all right, I had taken enough tranquilizers today to turn into an iceberg. But I knew I couldn't keep taking tranquilizers at this rate.

"Do you like subbing Mr. Johnson?" Cheryl asked.

"I don't know, this is only my second day."

The fourth period ended and my lunch period began.

I laid my head on the desk and went to sleep.

"Bzzzzzzzzzzz." The sixth period bell startled me. I lifted my head off the desk, I must have dozed off. Here they come!

"Yea, yea, we got a substitute!" a student started to jump up and down with glee.

The class came in and took their seats except for three wild looking young girls who approached my desk. They were up to something, I could tell in their faces. All three of the girls looked well developed for their ages, no doubt they should have been in high school by now. They all wore the tightest fitting dresses I'd seen in a while.

"Hi, I'm Candy." the first girl looked at me.

"I'm Joyce."

"I'm Lisa."

"Hi, I'm your substitute," I mimicked them in fun. My speech was starting to slur, I wondered if they noticed it.

"He's so cute," Candy giggled to Lisa.

"Will you be here at three?" Joyce asked.

"I guess I will, why?" The tranquilizers were allowing me to take all of this in stride.

"I'll be back." Candy said.

"Be back for what?"

"We want to go with you." Joyce was beginning to play with my mind. I was speechless.

"Why don't y'all go back to the projects where y'all belong." A male student in a yellow raincoat spoke up trying to come to my assistance. The three girls ignored him at first, but then Joyce told him to shut up.

"Aw I bet he can't do nothing." Candy said. I wondered how far they would go.

"I think you girls should have a seat."

"I had a sub one time, he couldn't do nothing," Lisa said arrogantly.

This type of talk from the female students caught me off guard.

"I told you girls to sit down!" I lost my cool.

"Sit us down!" Candy screamed.

I stood up slowly and eyed all three of them. I definitely couldn't let these girls intimidate me like this and get away with it.

"Don't you know we'll throw you out of that window!" Joyce said, arrogantly.

"Try it if you think you can do it!" I was ready for them, and besides, I glanced over at the window and wondered how they were going to throw me out of a window with metal bars on it.

After I said this they backed off and sat down. I presumed they were trying me out. Seeing that they couldn't intimidate me, they changed their tactics.

"Teach us something, you're supposed to be a teacher ain't you." Candy continued to agitate.

"You girls act like you know everything. What do you think I could teach you?"

They had gotten me started now, "and besides, I'm just your substitute for today. Your teacher didn't leave you an assignment. And further more I don't like your attitude anyway. I should send you three down to the office." The whole class was silent now, if I could have lit a match to the tension in the air it would have exploded. Everyone was guessing what the girls would say next. I was about to blow my top completely. These girls coming in here thinking they can push me around, this was me, C . J., I had been out there a little while.

I used to fight everyday when I was growing up. I mostly fought boys and then the next day, we were the best of friends. I only had to fight a girl once. And that was because I had beat up her brother. He ran and got his big sister who was 5 years older and twice as big as I was. I lost that fight but I wasn't planning on loosing anymore fights with girls. I didn't expect this much trouble from mere JUNIOR HIGH school students. Finally the three girls got up and walked out of the class room and normality returned.

"Bzzzzzzzzzzz," I was thankful What could happen next? I wondered what the seventh period would be like. I watched the students come in, and half of them were bigger than me. I was at the point now that I didn't care what the kids did so long as they didn't threaten me. I let them talk and curse each other and throw paper, trying to gain my composure from the previous period. I looked at the clock, 2:45, fifteen more minutes to go. Could I hold out just a little longer? Suddenly the whole class got up and walked out of the class room.

"Where are you people going? The bell hasn't sounded yet."

"Let us leave early Mr. Johnson, please," a female student begged.

"I can't, you know that. You're not supposed to leave out of here until the bell rings." I held my ground.

"We're leaving anyway," a short black, bald-headed boy said to me, "and you can't s top us!"

I decided to let them go, I was done for today, the sooner they were gone, the better. Inexplicably they returned. I was perplexed.

"I thought you people were gone. Why are you coming back?" I questioned as they broke their necks trying to get back in their seats.

"You busted on us Mr. Johnson." A student glared at me menacingly.

"What are you talking about?" I inquired.

"The principal caught us leaving, and you had to tell him."

"I didn't tell the principal anything, I was glad you were gone."

The principal came to the door. "Mr. Johnson, did you let this class out early?".

"No I didn't, I told them they couldn't leave until the bell rang, but they walked out anyway." I told the principal.

"All right, I want to see all of you at three o'clock, is that clear" The students just looked at the principal silently. The principal left and the short, black, bald-headed boy spoke up again.

"You busted on us, Mr. Johnson" the boy said as if singing a chant, "we're going to get you Mr. Johnson, we're going to get you!"

"'Bzzzzzzzzzzz" The three o'clock bell finally sounded. I didn't pay any attention to the boy's threat. I didn't worry, I hadn't told the principal they had left early, it was just a coincidence, the principal caught them leaving. I locked the door and went down to the office and turned in the key. It had been a day and a half. I wouldn't be able to take too much more of this. I walked down the hallway and saw the same short, black, bald-headed boy stop straight ahead of me near the office.

"I told you we were going to get you, didn't we," after he said that 40 students from the seventh period class converged around me. I was scared to death, these kids weren't playing. I looked around for some help, but the principal and security had disappeared into thin air. Time stopped. I stared at the short black, bald-headed boy, and he stared back at me. If they were going to get me, I was going to take one of them with me, and it was going to be that 'short, black, bald-headed boy' who was doing all of the talking. As suddenly as they had converged around me, they left from around me, and I stood in the hallway by myself, my heart in my stomach. I felt betrayed and abandoned. I looked at the administrators as if they were traitors. I left the school trying not to shake too much. But I didn't stop shaking until I drank two bottles of King Rose wine after I got home. I crawled into bed and fell asleep in a drunken stupor.

I awakened from my drunken stupor. It felt as if someone was choking me. I tried to move but I was paralyzed. I was starting to have trouble breathing. What was going on? Was I having a heart attack or stroke or something? Had someone broke in and tried to strangle me? Where was Karen?

I opened my eyes. Even though the bedroom was dimly lit by the moonlight that filtered in, I realized there was no one in the room but Karen and I. And she was fast asleep beside me. Yet I still felt as if someone was trying to strangle me and I still couldn't move. I began to feel an evil presence unlike anything I had ever experienced before. Then fear came over me. Had that student really sent a demon to kill me in my sleep?

I told myself I wasn't going out like that. With every once of strength I struggled to move. I was finally able to sit up in bed and breathe again. I no longer felt an evil presence. I put the whole episode out of my mind. It was just a bad dream, there were no such things as demons, right?

I took a sleeping pill and drifted off back to sleep.

4. Back To The New Grind

I had been substituting for a month. My first few days were rough, but things calmed down after that. But I still had my hands full on some days. Karen was working as a maid in a hotel, so that helped out. We were barely making it because I hadn't received my first pay check yet, the payroll system was one month behind so I didn't expect my check until the middle of October, a few days away.

    I looked over the Superintendant's memos and wondered if he was serious. If the kids went too far, I would defend myself, corporal punishment or not. I sat at the table in my worn house shoes and checkered house coat trying to sober up. I was up to two bottles of "King Rose Wine", a quart of beer, and three tranquilizers a day. I needed it to calm my nerves, but in the process my mind was slowly unraveling. I sipped on some bitter coffee and glanced through the bills. And on top of all the bills, I looked at the summons. We were two months behind in the rent.

    Could Karen and I keep up with the bills, plus accumulate enough money to pay off the bet with Matson? The way things looked, I either had to get a second job, probably at night, or get a hustle on the side. I ruled out a hustle on the side for the time being. That's what the bet was all about, that I could be successful without doing anything illegal. I glanced through the want ads for a second job.

The phone rang and I received my assignment for the day, one day, Science, Branner Junior High, Kovacks. I swallowed breakfast, a shot of 'King Rose' wine and two tranquilizers. I wondered how long I would be able to keep this pace up. There must be a better way. I dressed and went to the bus stop, unfortunately running into Matson on the way.

"Hey dude, what it look like?' Matson drawled as he stuck his bald head out the window of a '72 Cadillac. I looked at him with envy and subdued anger.

"Getting your money together?" He chuckled, like a hunter just before he springs the trap on his prey.

"Yeah, my bank account is getting pretty big," I lied like I didn't know what.

"Why are you walking then if you're making so much green?"
"I'm putting it all away in my bank account so I can make sure I'll win the bet." I continued to lie. Matson looked at me hard.

"I'll be checking with you dude, oh, by the way, I got some dynamite smoke and doujies, ya know."

"That's all right, I'll take a rain check," I replied. Matson nodded slyly and pulled off. I could have used a doujie in the state of mind I was in, but I knew I couldn't afford it. How did the name 'doujie' come about for dope? I understood why heroin was called dope. It would make you feel 'dopey' and high at the same time. But 'doujie', I couldn't figure that one. So much for my brief foray into the semantics of urban vernacular.

5. Assignment No. 17

I arrived at Banner late. They switched me to another class. Someone was already covering Kovac's class. I ended up covering a biology class, the teacher's name was Thomas, Thompson, or something they said. I walked into the classroom overhearing one student cursing another. It was going to be one of those days.

"You two cut that out, and watch your language." To my surprise, the students listened.

"Where's the money you owe me Beverly?" a male student in a green baseball cap asked another girl student. They were the only two students standing.

"I don't have it Sam." The girl looked toward me for assistance. Before I could speak, the boy grabbed the girl and started undressing her.

"You don't have my money! Well you're going to give something up. I started toward them as the boy continued to undress the girl, unbuttoning her blue and white blouse, and unzipping her red skirt. The girl didn't put up any resistance.

"Hold on now, I can't have you undressing a girl in class. If you want to do that, you'll have to do it somewhere else."

The two students left the classroom, the girl zipped her skirt back up on the way out. I didn't think they would actually take my advice, but they did to my amazement. The rest of the period went by uneventfully. I shook my head. If things got too crazy, I contacted the office, but more often than not, the call button didn't work and I had to deal with the situation on the spot, the best I could.

"RINGGGG", second period.

"Do you have any money?" A student asked me as the second period came in.

"No I don't," I told the truth. I was flat broke, all I had in my pocket was one bus token and two tranquilizers.

"Give me some money, I want some money." The student persisted.

"I told you I don`t have any money, now go over there and sit down." The student gave me a mischievous look and sat down.

Before I could take attendance, I saw what looked like fire coming from one of the student's desk. "Where's the smoke coming from?" I asked.

"They set the desk on fire, Mr. Johnson," a student said. I ran over to where I thought the smoke was coming from. The student who's desk was smoking just sat there and smiled.

"Why did you set that desk on fire? Get up and put it out." The student looked up at me and grinned.

"That's not smoke Mr. Johnson, that's just chalk dust from the erasers I clapped together to make you think it was smoke." The class burst out in laughter. I tried not to laugh. I shook my head again and sat down.

"Awwww!" I jumped up and felt my behind and pulled out a thumb tack.

"Ha, ha, ha,...." the Whole class laughed. I felt like a fool.

"All right, who put that tack in my chair!" I hollered. I felt so embarrassed.

"Bzzzzzzzzzz." The students left the room without answering my question. I braced myself for the third period. I remained standing as the third period class entered, I couldn't sit down yet. Before I could take a tranquilizer, I noticed a girl student come in with an egg in her hand. She walked toward me and stood beside me. The other students took their seats. "What are you going to do with that egg?" I looked at her, daring her not to even think about throwing it at me…

"Oh, nothing," she replied.

I turned away. The class started laughing. "What's so funny?" I asked the class. I turned back toward the girl who had the egg. She had somehow dropped it on herself and it was dripping from her blouse down to the floor.

"What happened to you?"

"I dropped the egg on myself," the girl said.

"Go wash yourself off and bring some paper towels back and clean that mess off the floor." I chuckled to myself. That's what she deserves. I let the class talk quietly among themselves for the remainder of the period.

"DINGGG." fourth period, lunch time. After the kids left I found my way to the teachers' lounge. Inside the lounge were three people, one young lady, in a purple pants suit, an older gentleman, and a young man, my age, about twenty three in a checkered sports coat.

"Hey, how are you," the young man greeted me, "Are you subbing today?"

"Yes, I am."

"Me too, how's your day been so far?"

"Kind of crazy, but I'm getting the hang of it." I sat down across from him. This was the first substitute I had a chance to speak to since I started.

"Those kids are terrible. I had one class where they talked about me like a dog. I used to yell at them, but when I got home, I was so tired and hoarse. So I don't yell anymore. I threw a chair at them one time, that's when they listened to me. I wish one of them would put a hand on me, I'd tear them up."

"Yeah, they will act crazy sometimes." I lit a cigarette and offered him one.

"Who're you in for?" the older gentleman inquired. "Thomas." I replied.

"Oh, you mean Thompson. How'd it go?"

"Kind of hectic, but I think I can handle it."

"I'm glad you're staying. The last sub they had for that class, the kids threw eggs at him and chased him down the hallway. He ran out the door and no one's seen him since."

"I won't let that happen to me," I boasted, "I'll run them out before they run me out." Or was that wishful thinking.

"I wish you luck." The man told me.

"DING DONG." Fifth period. I returned to my classroom. I had two more classes to go, the seventh period was my free period. I was glad of that, because I could leave early. The fifth period started off without incident, but I stayed on guard just in case. One boy got up and headed toward the door. "Where are you going?" I asked him sternly "Uhr,…uhrr, uhrrrrr..." the boy threw up on the floor before he could answer.

"Oooo, look at that, Ken threw up," a girl screeched as she turned her nose up.

"You better go to the nurse." The boy nodded and left the room.

"Somebody try and find the janitor so he can get this mess up off the floor."

"Can I go?" One boy shouted.

"Can I go?" Another boy asked.

"Let me go," a girl pleaded.

"You can go." I pointed to a student but they all ran out of the room.

"Open all of the windows," I choked as the room was beginning to smell, "open the doors too. Someone get some paper towels and put over it."

The students came back and told me they couldn't locate the janitor. They put paper towels over the mess. The odor had dissipated somewhat by now. I spent the rest of the period breathing through my mouth. Where could that janitor be? The sixth period bell sounded and still no janitor. The sixth period students came in and walked right into it.

"Watch your step." I cautioned. But it was too late.

"Why? What's that on the floor?" a student asked.

"A boy threw up ."

"Guuuush, pew," a boy said as he took a wide detour around the mess on the floor. I sent another student to find the janitor again. He returned and said the janitor would clean it up at three o'clock. That would be a big help. I needed it cleaned up now. I stepped out into the hallway for a moment to get some fresh air, almost colliding with several students running down the hallway hollering and screaming.

"Come back here:" A hall monitor yelled.

In a few moments the students turned the corner and disappeared with the hall monitor hot on their tracks.

"Pow, boom, blam, bump, plow, blap, blap!!"

I rushed back into the classroom.

A boy and girl were fighting like cats and dogs.

"Blap, blam, boom." They were going at it, knocking chairs and desks over. Students crowded around and urged them on. I ran toward them and grabbed the girl and tried to pull her off the boy. She dug her fingernails into his face and left a scratch on his face from his under his eye down to his neck.

"Break it up," I tussled with the girl, trying to pull her away, "break it up." She was a wild one. I managed to get one of her arms free, I reached for her other arm but slipped in the throw up. As I fell to the floor I pulled the girl down with me and she in turn pulled the boy down. We were all slipping and sliding in the throw up. I couldn't pull the girl away from that boy for anything. I was relieved when security came in and helped me pull the girl off the boy. We finally separated them.

"What happened?" the security person asked.

"I'd just stepped outside the classroom for a few seconds and the next thing I knew they were at each other's throats." I shivered as I tried to wipe some of the throw up off of my hands. The seventh period bell signaled, none too soon.

"I'll take care of these two. Are you all right?"

"Yeah," I answered, "all I need now is a good hot bath."
I was a stinking mess. Thank goodness my seventh period was a free period. I left the school totally disgusted. As I walked down the school yard I felt something hard poke me in my back.

"Stick 'em up!" I heard a voice say from behind me, and the voice sounded familiar. I stopped dead in my tracks.

"Wait a minute, weren't you in my second period class?" I couldn't believe one of my students was trying to rob me. I waited for an answer but there was none. I turned around and it was the same boy in my second period class that had asked me for some money. I looked at him and he looked at me, grinning.

"I was just fooling," he said and ran down the street. I popped both tranquilizers in my mouth and headed for the nearest liquor store for a bottle of 'King Rose'. But it didn't dawn on me until I got to the store that all I had in my pocket was one bus token. I turned around and headed for a bus stop. Passersby looked at me strangely, wondering why I was smelling so bad.

6. The Last Straw

I awoke early. I was sweating profusely. I had just snapped out of a nightmare. I dreamed that I had stepped into the class-room and started falling into some kind of hole in the floor. All I remembered hearing were the kids' laughter as I felt myself falling. I pondered the meaning of the dream. There had to be a better way, but what was it?

The tranquilizers weren't doing me any good lately. No doubt my tolerance had built up. I was taking sleeping pills to get to sleep and pep pills to get going. I was up to about three bottles of 'King Rose' a day now. I found I couldn't even get through a day without the pills. Karen and I had finally caught up with our rent and bills. I was finally able to save up a hundred dollars in the bank. But it was getting near Christmas so I doubted if the money would be there long. I glanced at the clock, 6:30AM. Karen was still sleep. She should have been gone.

"Karen, Karen," I reached over and shook her.

"What, what. What is it?" she grumbled as she opened her eyes.

"Are you going to work today? It's 6:30."

"I quit that job Cornell. I can't get up early anymore. Don't worry, I'll find another job where I don't have to get up so early," she finished and went back to sleep.

She picked a fine time to stop working. Just as we were getting on our feet and near Christmas too at that. I tried to go back to sleep, but couldn't. So I laid in the bed contemplating getting a second job. I reminded myself to call the Purple Giraffe Restaurant where I had worked as a dishwasher last year. I was sure the manager would let me work there again in the evenings part time. I knew we needed some extra money around this time of year, it was only about a week and a half before Christmas. The phone rang and I got my first extended assignment, four days, General Math, Crampton Junior High, for Bullock. I dressed and gulped down a fast breakfast and left the apartment. On the bus I saw Jimmy sitting in the back. I made my way toward him.

"Hey C.J., what you go say?" Jimmy said as I sat down beside him.

Jimmy had a restrained expression on his tired face.

"Not too much. I'm on my way to work." I glanced out the window and for a moment I thought I saw some snow flakes.

"Where are you headed?" I asked.

"Down to the pool room to make me some cash. You heard about Matson?" Jimmy's eyes-probed mine for a reaction.

"Naw, what about him?"

"He got busted on a drug charge."

I felt a sense of relief, maybe things would turn out right after all.

"I'm sorry to hear that," I had become an expert liar.

"I guess you feel kind of lucky." Jimmy said sarcastically.

"Why?"

"You might not have to pay off the bet." Jimmy smirked.

"You know about the bet?" I was surprised the word had travelled so fast.

"The whole neighborhood knows about it." Jimmy said half jokingly.

The bus neared my stop. "I'll catch you later Jimmy."

"Later," he replied.

Crampton was one of the new schools that had been built a few years ago. I entered the classroom after checking in at the office. I didn't have a homeroom class for a change.

"ZINGGGGGGG." First period.

"Are you the substitute?" a girl in a brown jacket asked.

"Yes, I'm, Mr. Johnson."

"Do you believe in God?"

Here we go again. Why do these students keep asking me that?

"What does it matter if I believe in God or not. Will that change anything for you or for me?" My minor in philosophy had made me quite the skeptic.

"Do you believe in salvation," another student asked. There was something about this student that I couldn't put my finger on.

"Do I believe in what?" I was confused.

"Do you believe in salvation through Jesus Christ?" the student's words were penetrating.

"Leave him alone Stephanie," another student interrupted," "We're not in church."

"Tell me more Stephanie," I urged her to continue despite another student's objection.

"If you confess with your mouth the Lord Jesus and believe in your heart that God has raised him from the dead, you will be saved."

"Mr. Johnson?" Another girl in pigtails asked sharply.

"Yes."

"Tell us something about sex."

"What do you want to know?" I was glad they asked me about something I knew a little about. I couldn't get with this Jesus thing.

"Just tell us something about it."

"Tell you something about it, uh. You have regular or heterosexual relations, homosexuality, bestiality, voyeurism, exhibitionism, sodomy, lesbianism, nymphomania, satyriasis, bisexuals, eunuchs, virgins and aphrodisiacs."

The students were speechless. I didn't know what had gotten in to me, but I figured I'd give them some answers to last them for a while.

"Can we jump some rope?" A girl asked.

Before I could answer, two girls stood up and started turning a rope. A few other girls formed a line and began jumping rope in turn. I just looked at them and said, "you people having fun?"

"Are you having fun?" A girl asked.

"RINGGGGGGGGGG." second period.

"Can we play some cards Mr.?" a boy asked as he came in.

"I guess it'll be all right, if you do it quietly." I thought that would keep them occupied. I watched them. I didn't notice anything unusual until I heard something hit the floor, like dice bouncing. I walked to the back of the room and caught two boys shooting craps.

"You can't do that in here," I said, "give me the dice." They complied.

I looked over the card game and saw money on the desks. "Give me the cards too. I thought you people were going to play for fun, not money." I took the cards and dice and sat down at my desk. No sooner had I sat down, I saw a small rubber football sail across the room.

"Stop playing ball in here, this is not a football field," I said, to no avail. The students continued to throw the football back and forth across the room. Someone threw the football a little too high and it hit a light. The light shattered and the football sailed out of the open window.

"I guess you're satisfied now, you broke a light." I said.

A boy jumped up, "I'll get it."

"Leave it out there," I said as the boy sat back down.

"BINGGG..." Third period, my free period. I located the teacher's lounge after the students left. I couldn't help but to ponder Stephanie's religious question about salvation. Was someone trying to tell me something? I came in and sat down, the other teachers didn't seem to even notice me, unless they were ignoring me intentionally.

"It's terrible," one of the teachers continued, "they threw a teacher out of a second floor window over at Spinley."

"What?" the other teacher remarked in disbelief.

"Sure did. The teacher was hospitalized. Her husband's taking the kids to court who did it. I heard that some of those kids dropped a desk out of the window and it almost hit the principal in the head."

I was listening to their conversation intensely, I hoped I didn't ever get an assignment at that school.

"I knew this one teacher who used to work there. She told me that when she first started she used to carry her gun to school with her."

"Does Miss Pickens still work there?" The teacher asked the other.

"No, some students tossed a brick through her door window when she was pregnant and she didn't come back. They used to do all kinds of things at that school, set the bathroom on fire, throw firecrackers down ventilators and set off smoke bombs and stink bombs in the hallways and in some classrooms. They used to beat the principal up over there, too. Got so bad, he was afraid to come out of his office during school hours.

"Yeah, Carol, those students can get out of hand at times. I had a student the other day pull a knife on another student after they'd practically cursed each other out several times over."

"Did you hear about a teacher getting raped over at Cummings Tech the other day?" Carol continued, "in the counselor's office?"

"No, I haven't heard about that." The other teacher shifted in her seat, her expression became more serious.

"It happened after school."

"RINNGGG." Fourth period. I returned to my room. The first to enter the room was a small dog, followed by a little boy, who couldn't have been more than three years old. A girl followed them with the rest of the class.

I chased the dog out of the room and watched it run down the hall. I looked at the girl who by now had picked up the little boy in her arms. I looked behind her and saw a girl who looked like she was pregnant, she couldn't have been more than fourteen years old.

"Do they allow you to bring children to school?" I asked the girl, feeling sympathy toward her and the pregnant girl behind her. They sure were starting out young now.

"I couldn't find anyone to take care of my baby today, so I brought him with me," she said.

"Pardon this interruption," came a voice over the wall intercom, "if there are any children in the building, please take them out of the building. No small children should be in building."

Things settled down for the rest of the period, I counted the minutes for the next bell.

"Plow:" I was startled. It sounded as if someone had tried to kick the door off its hinges. I jumped up and ran toward the door, then looked down the hall. Whoever it had been, they were gone by now.

The fifth period bell sounded. I noted on my schedule that I was to cover a music class this period. I locked the doors and walked through the hallway toward the music room. When I got there, the door was already open and I could hear the jagged cacophony of the kids banging randomly on the piano.

I walked in and sat down. I began to feel as if I was running out of steam so I inconspicuously swallowed a pep pill to keep going.

"Are you our substitute?" a student asked.

"Yes, I am for this period. I'm Mr. Johnson."

"Can we listen to the record player?" Another student asked. I saw no harm in it. "Yes you can. You know how to cut it on?" I Asked.

"Yeah," a student exclaimed as he ran over to the record player and put a record on. The next thing I knew, a light-skinned shapely girl jumped up on top of my desk and began to do a shake dance to the music. She was shaking all she had right in my face. I became mesmerized at her gyrations. The rest of the class cheered her on as she simulated the bumps and grinds of a strip tease act.

The record finally played out and the girl started laughing hysterically and jumped from my desk. As if this was some kind of a signal, the rest of the class commenced to bang on the piano, blow whistles, crash the symbols, blow horns, beat on drums and shake tambourines. At this point I felt a slight surge of energy and knew the pep pill was beginning to work. Unfortunately, the sound became more amplified to me than it really was, because the pep pill stimulated my whole nervous system. Now it gave me the jitters.

I sent a boy to go and get the principal. "You people can keep on making all this racket because I've already sent somebody to get the principal."

After I said this they quieted down for the moment. They confined their noise making to banging on the piano. The boy I had sent to get the principal never came back. No doubt he had decided to go awol.

"RINNGGGGG..." Sixth period. The students left the room as I looked beside the desk for my briefcase, but it was gone. I looked all over the music room and even went back to the other classroom and looked. I couldn't find my briefcase anywhere. That was the last straw. Those maniacs had stolen my briefcase. I had some important papers and the last of my sleeping pills in it, and that's what burned me up. I grabbed my coat and walked out of that wild school, even though I had two more periods to go. I told myself I wasn't coming back to sub anymore.

As I walked down the street, I heard someone calling from the school window, "Hey Mr., Mr....", but I kept walking, I didn't even want to look back.

"Stephanie's words continued to echo in my mind," "Salvation through Jesus, salvation through Jesus..." But I never could accept the idea of a savior dying on a cross for our sins. It just didn't make sense to me. Why would God allow his son to die on a cross for us? It wasn't logical. Now Kant's 'Critique of Pure Reason', that was logical. I liked Emmanuel Kant's words, 'cogito, ergo sum', I think, therefore I am. My words were, I C.J., therefore I win.

7. Pawn to King Rook Four

I saw the manager at the Purple Giraffe. It was a well-travelled uptown joint with a purple and white giraffe over the entrance. Lou said he would be glad to let me work part time there again. He said I could start tomorrow night.

I called Karen and told her I was at the Purple Giraffe and that I would be a little late getting home. I had a difficult time explaining to her that I was working a second job and not seeing another woman. Why couldn't she understand?

I really didn't want to keep subbing but I needed the money. I called in the next morning and asked for any other school except Crampton. The only thing they said they had left was a three day assignment at Spinley. I took it, forgetting that Spinley was the school where a teacher had been thrown out of a window. I walked cautiously into the classroom, after signing in at the office. I didn't bring a briefcase this time, they wouldn't steal another one from me. I stuffed my coat into the desk drawer. I figured that if someone tried to steal my coat, I would catch them.

I sat back and considered my situation. With Matson in jail, I could relax a little and regroup. I took some mail out of my pocket. I opened four envelopes containing a returned job application, two pieces of junk mail and the phone bill. The money Karen and I made before Christmas would not be counted toward fulfilling the bet. That money had to go to gifts and other items. I resigned myself to the inevitability of having to start fresh in January saving money.

I computed my gross salary if I were to work everyday from September to June. I then figured my gross from my part time job, if I had it that long. I figured that after deductions, I would take home something like $4500. I subtracted my expenses. What was left, was far short of the thousand dollars I would need if I lost the bet. I would have to encourage Karen to get another job.

I needed a way to make more money. I also had the option of either working or drawing unemployment or both during the summer months until next September. That would help out considerably. With Matson in jail, I thought about doing a little hustling of my own. I would have to make sure Matson didn't find out about it.

Then I realized what I should do. Wait for word on Matson's trial, if he was convicted, I wouldn't have anything to worry about. If he got off, things would get tricky. As I contemplated a safe hustle, if there was such a thing, my homeroom section trickled into the room.

After taking the roll, the first period started. I noticed one student with a chess board in his hand as he entered the room.

"Are you a chess player?" I asked the student.

"Sure, I am. You want to play me a game?"

"Yes I do," I said as we began to set up the chessboard. A few of the students gathered around as we started to play. I gave the student the edge of playing with the white pieces. His first opening move was a ridiculous king rook pawn to king rook four. That move was a popular one among inexperienced players. I proceeded, after moving my king pawn to king four, to execute an attack on his weakest point, his king bishop two square, with my bishop and queen. In a few more moves I completed a 'fool's mate' on him. The student looked at the board in disbelief. He wondered how I was able to checkmate him so fast.

"You want to play another game?" I was starting to have some fun.

"Naw."

"I'll play you, a second student spoke up. I thought I would not demoralize this student by beating him too fast. After getting my king knight and king bishop off of the back rank, I castled on the king side.

"What was that move?" The second student asked. "That's castling on the king's side."

"I never saw a move like that."

"He can do that," another boy verified my move, "that's called castling."

"I still don't believe he can do that," the boy insisted. "Ha, ha, ha," the boy chucked, "you're just mad because you're losing."

"Who are you laughing at?" The boy stopped playing and jumped up.

"You!"

Here we go again. The two boys starting flailing away at each other. I finally separated them. These students seemed to want to fight at the drop of a hat.

"DINNGGG." Second period. To my surprise, not one student entered my room after the first fifteen minutes. I looked in the teacher's desk drawer and pulled out two books. The first was titled, I WAS A STRAIGHT-LACED NYMPHO, and the second was titled, HOT BUTTERED LOVE. I flicked through the papers and books on the desk in an effort to kill some time. Sometimes the period went by so slow. I doodled and flipped through the magazines a second time.

"RINNGGGGG." I looked on the schedule and noticed the Christmas assembly was starting now. I went to the assembly and listened to Christmas carols sung by the chorus.

What was Christmas all about? I asked myself A time to sing songs and carols about some man called Jesus, and then go home or party and get so high and drunk that we then want to shot and cut one another. It just seemed to me to be another time of the year for people to have an excuse to steal and rip each other off and hurt each other. It had become so commercialized. Just another pagan holiday, I thought. The Muslims said it was really a celebration of Nimrod's birthday. I couldn't believe Jesus was the son of God and I didn't see how anyone could live by the bible. But just in case it was true, I tried to keep some of the commandments. I wasn't a complete heathen.

After the assembly, I went to lunch. After lunch, the fifth period started. I introduced myself to the class and decided to put some problems on the board to keep them busy. After I put the problems on the board, I smelled smoke from a cigarette.

"Put that cigarette out. You're not allowed to smoke in here." I yelled.

The student took one more puff off the cigarette and then took his time putting it out. Four boys left their seats and stood around my desk. I wondered what they were up to. All of a sudden they lifted the desk up and tried to turn it over on me. I slid out of the way just in time as the desk went crashing to the floor sideways. The boys then ran out the room.

"Does anyone know those boys' names?" I asked, astonished at what the boys had tried to do.

"No, they didn't belong in here." The sixth period bell clanged. About five minutes went by and no class, but they finally straggled in. As the class sat down, all was quiet until I heard the crack of a portable radio coming on.

"Hot dog! Let's have some music!" one boy shouted as he began to snap his fingers to the music. Suddenly two girls jumped up and started dancing with each other. Then another boy jumped up and started to do some fancy footwork.

I just sat back and watched the whole spectacle. Before I asked someone to get the principal, I reconsidered. These kids weren't hurting anyone, they were just having a little fun. I allowed them to continue dancing, but the music was too loud, so I told them to turn it off.

"Mr. Johnson, please report to the office, it's important." came the words over the intercom. I left the classroom and went down to the office and was directed to a room in the rear. I stepped into the room and saw a policeman, another slender-looking man, the assistant principal and a student with tears in his eyes. I recognized the student as one who had been in my fifth period.

"This student says another boy took his money from him in your class," The assistant principal stated.

"What? I didn't see anyone take his money. What's going on?" I was puzzled.

"Darrell, didn't you say someone took your money in this teacher's class?" the boy's father asked.

"Yeah."

"Tell us how it happened," the assistant principal urged him. "What was the teacher doing while the boy took your money?"
I swallowed hard, wondering if this was some kind of set-up.

"His back was turned. He was writing something on the board."

"Why didn't you tell the teacher the boy took your money, Darrell?" His father asked him curiously. Darrell just hung his head down, not speaking.

"All right Mr. Johnson, that's all we just wanted to know what happened up there."

I nodded my head in relief and returned to my classroom. For the first time I began to have doubts about this substitute job, and doubts about the school system in general. More so than I did before. I was still shocked that so much had happened when I turned my back for a few seconds. I realized that these students would have to be watched more closely. I figured that the boy didn't tell me because he was probably afraid the other boy would beat him up. But I was still amazed that the boy had gotten robbed so quickly without me knowing.

I reentered the classroom and sat down. What kind of school was this? What kind of substitute was I to allow something like that to take place? But it wasn't my fault, it couldn't have been my fault. The boy didn't even tell me what had happened, how was I to know? I couldn't possibly be to blame. But somehow I still felt responsible.

The seventh period bell echoed. The playful students soon filtered in. Ten minutes later, I had a total of four students in my seventh period class.

"Where is the rest of the class?" I stood up and looked about the almost vacant room.

"Most of them either went home or to the school dance," a student answered, looking out the window with detachment. "Where is the school dance being held?"

"In the gym."

"Why didn't you students go?"

"We don't have a quarter. It cost a quarter to get in."

I assumed the student was telling the truth. I reached in my pocket and pulled out some change. "Here's a quarter for each one of you." I said as they grabbed the money from my hands. "Now you all can go to the dance."

The four students left the room. I looked at the clock two thirty, and contemplated leaving for home. I gathered my coat and started toward the door. A student came back into the room.

"What happened? I thought I gave you a quarter to go to the dance? Why are you back?"

."I was running down the steps and the quarter fell out of my hands. I looked all over for it but couldn't find it." The student told me in a serious tone.

I thought for a second, was the student trying to con me or not. His story didn't sound too likely, so he and I remained in the classroom looking at each other until three o'clock. I popped a pep pill to make sure I had enough energy to keep going and went to my part-time job at the PURPLE GIRAFFE.

8. Day Two, Spinley Junior High School

I had finally persuaded Karen to go back to work. This time she found herself an office job as a file clerk. I hoped she would keep it longer than the first one she had. Through the grapevine I had gathered that Matson was out on bond with his trial coming up next month. So I would still be in the dark until then concerning his fate. I stopped telling Karen about any incidents involving any female students, she said she didn't want to hear about it.

I reconsidered a side hustle until hopefully Matson was behind bars. Having a hustle on the side would go against my philosophy, that I could make more money legally and win the bet. I decided to stay with my original philosophy and rule out a side hustle.

I popped a pep pill to get going again and went back to Spinley for my second round. A skinny dark boy came in and looked at me strangely, put his book bags down and walked back out the room as my first period started. In a few moments he returned to harass me.

"You took two dollars out of my book bag Mr." The boy accused me harshly. I wondered to myself, was he for real?

"What are you talking about? I didn't take anything out of your book bag." I looked at him, trying to fathom his intentions.

"You did too take some money from my book bag I had two dollars in it, and now it's gone." He came toward me, in a threatening manner. I braced myself for a confrontation, my pulse increased slightly.

"You better give me my money back." The boy tried to intimidate me as the rest of the class looked on intently.

"You better sit down boy." I was beginning to get angry.

"I want my money." He insisted.

"I'm telling you for the last time, I don't have your money."

The boy stopped accusing me of taking his money and went to the blackboard and played tic-tac-toe with himself. I looked at the boy. I speculated on what hospital he had just gotten out of.

Two tall boys peered in the door and then came in.

"Are you two supposed to be in this class." I questioned them.

"Hell No!"

"I suggest you go to where you belong."

"We're not going anywhere."

"Oh yes you are. I'm not going to let you disrupt my class." I moved toward them quickly. I pushed them both out of the room. One of the boys decided to get indignant and swung at me. Now why did he want to do that? I swung wildly and luckily landed a blow to his head and he reeled back. The other boy came from behind and jumped on my back and wrapped his arms around my throat. I struggled to get free, but couldn't.

By this time the rest of my class had crowded around us, edging us on, yelling "Fight! Fight!"

The boy I had hit regained his balance and lunged toward me. I put my foot out and kicked him squarely in his abdomen. He grabbed his midsection and buckled over in pain. I dropped down to my knees and flipped the other boy over off my back, and he hit the floor. Just as I started to kick both of them in the behind, they got up and ran down the hallway and out of sight. Another teacher came running toward me.

"Are you all right Mr.?"

"Yeah, I'm fine, just fine." I brushed myself off and told my class to get back in the room, the excitement was over and so was the period.

"Rinnnnggg."

"I don't think they even go to this school," the teacher said, "sometimes we have trouble with outsiders."

"I'll try to be on the look out," I said as I waited for my second period class. The second period came in almost too quietly and took their seats. A few minutes later, a student began to talk about me, about the way I looked, anything he could find.

"What kind of shoes you got on Mr.?" A smart student asked.

"Regular shoes. What kind of shoes do you think they are?"

"They look like specs to me." The student continued. "Look at his pants," he told another student, "he's got some bama pants on."

I fumed in my seat, calculating his next remark.

"Where are you from?" He asked.

"You figure it out." I started to lose my patience.

He knew he was getting to me. "Hey look at that man's head, he's got a peanut-shaped head. Don't he?" He asked the rest of the class.

"And look at his lips, they all cracked." The class erupted into boisterous laughter, I was silent and becoming angry.

"What's your name boy?" I asked.

"My name? My name is Bobo Brazil."

The class erupted into laughter again.

"Quiet down, I've had enough of this." I motioned to another student. "Go down and get the principal." But no one moved.

"Oh, that's the way it's going to be. Well I'll go down and get him myself," I said as I left the room. Before I could get down the steps, the bell rang, for the third period which was my free period. I walked to the lounge. I needed a short break. I entered the lounge and started talking to an attractive young teacher who dressed like a gypsy and talked like a secretary.

"I used to work in private industry," she said scrutinizing my reaction. "But I got bored with the job during the day and got tired of partying all night and trying to go in the next day. That's why I decided to teach. There's always something going on. And if they act up I tell them that I teach social studies and not home training. That's if they don't know how to act, for them to get out. I've been here for a while, long enough to have a pretty good reputation. It helps a lot in a school like this."

"I guess it does," I glanced around the lounge at a broken soda machine, then glanced back at her. She continued:

"We have an inefficient superintendent. There's a shortage of everything, books, teachers' aides, learning materials for special classes. They are cutting back on staff. Our teachers' union is threatening to strike after Christmas if they don't get things straightened out and stop the cut backs. All the school board seems to be interested in is budget restrictions and economizing. We haven't had a pay raise in two years. The way things look, we'll have to go on strike."

"I guess we substitutes will be used as strike breakers," I said in a joking manner. She looked at me, irritated by what I had said. It wasn't a joking matter to her. A teacher's strike was something I hadn't considered. I was all for teachers and their grievances, but when it came to the money, I probably would cross the picket lines. I had to survive. You have to do what you have to do. Abruptly the young woman left the lounge. A few minutes later, another young man entered the room. I could smell alcohol on his breath.

"They're something, ain't they?" He asked me for my confirmation. "Yeah, they sure are."

"I always have my drink before I get here. And I have a few more at lunch time. Only way I can make it," he said.

I was glad that I wasn't the only one who had a few every now and then.

"I had a problem keeping some students from jumping on a student in my class who was gay. And another boy was criticizing this boy because he hadn't had sex yet. How's your day been?"

"I was attacked by some outsiders, other than that, it hasn't been too bad." I lit a cigarette.

He paused and looked at me sympathetically. The next instant we were interrupted by frantic pleas from an elderly man who had come in.

"Come and get 'em, come and get 'em. I can't handle them anymore. They're jumping on the desks and everything." A retired teacher turned substitute croaked.

"Excuse me, I'll see you later," the young man said to me as he went to the man's assistance.

"Rinnngggg." Fourth period. Back in class, I sat and awaited the onslaught. They came in more orderly than I expected and took their seats. I watched one boy get up and sit down beside a girl and begin fondling and kissing her. I watched for a moment and then spoke,

"Why don't you wait until you leave class before you do that?" The boy looked at me and smiled, and returned to his seat.

I turned and saw a magazine fly across the room, then another, and another. I thought I'd try something new. I saw a paddle on the desk. I picked it up and headed for the nearest student who was throwing the magazines. I whacked him a few with the paddle and he settled down. I was taking a chance because I wasn't supposed to be using corporal punishment.

"I want you people to behave and stop throwing those magazines or I'll use this stick on you."

At once the whole class stopped throwing the magazines. I told myself I would use a paddle more often, it really seemed to work. The kids' parents should discipline them at home before they got to school. But the way things went, it seemed as if the teacher had to teach students manners and respect.

As the fifth period started, I took my lunch period. I really was feeling down. I called Lou and told him I didn't feel well and wouldn't be in. I munched on a cheese and bologna sandwich, but my appetite was gone. I decided to call Karen.

"Hello, may I speak to Miss Karen Bailey please."

"Just a minute," a voice on the other end said.

"Hello Cornell," Karen's voice was on the line now.

"Yeah, how are you doing? How's the new job?" I asked.

"It's coming along fine so far. Except sometimes I get tired standing on my feet. I have to stand up a while at the X-Y-Z files. Other than that, I'm doing all right here. How about you? How are the kids treating you today?"

"I got jumped by two boys who didn't belong in the building, other than that, it hasn't been anything out of the ordinary much." I tried to light a cigarette with one hand while my other hand was holding the receiver, but this was an impossible task.

"Cornell, why don't you find some other kind of work. I don't see how you're going to make enough money to win the bet with Matson if you keep substituting. I don't like you being around all those women teachers anyway.

"Now you know you are the only one for me. You don't have to worry about me liking anybody else, you know that Karen." I was definitely in love with Karen but I had difficulty expressing it to her. But I think she sensed how I felt even though I didn't always say it.

"Do you love me Cornell?" Karen inquired.

"Of course I do. You know I do." I responded. I couldn't come out and say the word, l-o-v-e, but I could agree with her.

"I don't feel well today, I'm not going in to the Purple Giraffe, I'll be home early today, see you then," I sent her a kiss over the phone.

"Bye Cornell," she sent me a kiss back. I hung up and returned to class. Maybe Karen was right, I did need to find another job. It just didn't look like I was going to make enough money substituting. But I had tried to find other jobs all over, but nothing came through. Every time I didn't get a particular job I had applied for, I would hit the bottle and pills even harder. It was getting to the point where I was almost afraid to apply for another position.

I feared rejection, depression, and what I didn't want to admit, feeling sorry for myself. There must be a better way, but what was it? When I was younger, I read all kinds of books, philosophy, psychology, science, thinking that the more I read, the better equipped I would be to deal with life.

I thought if I made myself so smart, I would be able to do anything I wanted to do. I would make a lot of money, have all the women, be on top of the world. It hadn't quite worked out that way. It seemed I could read everything except the bible. Every time I picked the bible up, I would put it down after reading a few verses because it didn't seem to make any sense.

The god the philosophers talked about seemed to be just a mere abstraction, an omnipotent god yes, but a god off in the distance somewhere. The god of the philosophers couldn't help me with my problems, the philosopher's god seemed to only exist in their minds. Everyone in the church seemed to be either gay or hypocrites. God had to be more than what the philosophers said he was, but how could I find him? How could I get to know what he really was like? If he did exist.

Was Jesus the answer after all? I wondered. I had attended Sunday school when I was a kid, but when I got out of Sunday school, I didn't see anyone living the so-called Christian life. So I stopped going to Sunday school, thinking it was a waste of time. I couldn't understand why if there was a God, why did he allow so many terrible things to happen in the world.

I felt secure when I substituted. After all, it was a job and it was better than nothing. Secondly, when I got to school, despite the kids' behavior, it took my mind off my problems. I was so busy trying to deal with them that I forgot all about my own. Thirdly, at the rate I was drinking and popping pills, I wondered if I was good for anything else.

Where was my self confidence? This was me, C. J. I had to get myself together. I had to snap out of this state of mind. This wouldn't do at all, I told myself. And at the back of my mind eating away like a cancer, was the ever present feeling of impending doom if I didn't win the bet with Matson. I hoped and hoped they would throw the book at him in court. Why did I ever make the bet with him in the first place? What was I trying to prove?

The sixth period bell echoed. I looked out of the window and saw snow falling. I watched two boys come toward my desk. One of them held out what looked like a switchblade.

"Have you ever seen one of these?" The boy asked.

I kept my eye on the knife and answered: "Yes, I have."

"You ever been cut by one of these?" The boy asked.

I tried not to look afraid, I answered him in a tense voice.

"No."

The boy pushed the button and the blade snapped out, I just looked at the knife. I didn't make any sudden moves. The boy, seeing that I didn't panic, put the knife away and left the room with the other student.

As they left, I heard one of them say, "ha, ha, ha, he was scared to death wasn't he? Ha,ha."

Some of those students sure had a morbid sense of humor. I looked around the classroom. The class hadn't even paid any attention to the incident, as if it happened everyday. I looked down at the roll and then heard something hit the glass window beside me. I looked at the window and the remnants of snowball were trickling down the still-intact window pane. I got up and headed to the door. I looked out and saw no one in the halls. I asked the class, "did anyone see who threw that snowball at me?"

"No, we didn't." No one wanted to tell me anything. I went back to the desk and remained on my guard. As soon as I settled down, a tan-complexioned boy came running through the door. And behind him came the assistant principal.

"Come back here boy, don't run from me." The assistant principal ran after the boy. I looked on in amazement. The assistant principal finally cornered the boy in the back of the class. He grabbed the boy and unleashed three successive blows to the boy's chest. The boy struggled to get away from the assistant principal's grasp. The other students in the class cried out, "Hit him Mr. Pennington, hit him again." Mr. Pennington hit the boy again and then led him out the room, apologizing for the disturbance.

"How's your day been?" Mr. Penington asked me.

"A little intense, but I'm still in one piece," I mused.

The assistant principal chuckled and left the room, and then came back. "Oh, could you cover room 308 next period. Your seventh period class has been excused.

"Yes, I can," I said as I prepared to leave the room.

"Rinnnggg." Seventh period. I walked to room 308 and the first thing I noticed about the room were the holes in the ceiling. I watched the seventh period class come in. I had forgotten to ask the assistant principal what subject this was.

"What subject is this?" I asked a student calmly.

"This is a Health class," a student answered. As I started to count the minutes until three o'clock, three students left their seats, and climbed up on top of the cabinet and into and through the holes in the ceiling. The rest of the class looked up.

"Awwww, y'all are going to get in trouble," a girl shouted as the boys started dropping bits of plaster on top of the other student's heads and on top of mine.

"Come down out of that ceiling!" I yelled to no avail as I could hear them crawling about over my head. I knew that if one of them fell from the ceiling, I would be blamed. "Well, you have to come down sometime, by that time I'll have the principal here," I warned them.

"No, they don't," a student spoke up.

"What do you mean?"

"They can crawl to the bathroom up there. The bathroom has holes in the ceiling too." A student explained.

I ran out the room toward the bathroom in an effort to try to catch the students before they dropped down from the bathroom ceiling, but I was too late. When they saw me coming, they crawled back up into the ceiling, crawled back to the class room, dropped down and ran out the door before I could get back. I looked at the roll and by a process of elimination turned in the names to the office of the boys who had been crawling in the ceiling dropping plaster down.

"Ding...." three o'clock, the day was finally over.

9. The Thin Red Line

I didn't feel well at all when I got home. I went straight to bed. I couldn't fall asleep, I was restless for some reason. Karen came home and asked me how I felt, and I told her, terrible.

"You stay in bed and cover up and rest," she said as she fixed something for me to eat.

"You don't have to cook anything Karen, I'm not hungry. I'm just going to sleep," I said as I swallowed two sleeping pills and sat back. I drifted off to sleep.

I dragged myself out of bed, thankful that today was the last day of school before the holidays. I really didn't feel up to going to work, but I knew that I had to carry out my assignment or else chance a negative notation in my substitute record.

I left the apartment and went to Spinley for the third and I hoped, last time. I looked in the desk and gathered up as many ditto sheets as I could find. I would try to keep them busy with the sheets. There was an assembly in the morning. I took my homeroom down and seated them in the auditorium, then I took my seat at the end of the row.

"Good morning, students, visitors, parents and faculty. I welcome everyone this morning to our Athletic assembly." The principal greeted the audience. On his right were two gym teachers, and on his left a large gold trophy.

"You people came into this auditorium pretty good this time. I'm glad that I didn't have to send anyone back. I am proud to announce that Spinley, won first place in the hundred yard dash, second place in the five hundred meter relay, and we won first place in the poll vaulting contest."

The audience clapped with approval. I was still trying to wake up. The two gym teachers presented the trophy to the principal and to the school. The principal then went on to explain how important grades were in choosing a student to participate in athletics, and how strong Spinley's sports program was. After wishing us a merry holiday he dismissed the students to their second period class. I returned to the classroom and awaited the second period. A boy entered the room with his coat on and kicked the trash can across the room. He was followed by two other boys with coats on. I played it by ear.

"Do you have to kick the trash can when you come into the room?" I asked.

"It was an accident." The student snapped.

"Have it your way," I was annoyed at his manner.

"Are you going to be our new teacher?" One of the boys asked.

"No, I'm just the substitute today." I began to smell something burning in the hallway.

"What's that I smell?"

The boys didn't answer. I soon recognized the aroma, it was marijuana. I went out into the hallway and saw a few students walking down the hall, but none of them were smoking.

"It's probably coming from the bathroom," a boy spoke.

"Where's the rest of the class?" I enquired.

"They're in the halls I think," a boy answered. Several students came in the class, then walked back out. They were taking advantage of the holiday season, roaming the halls at will.

The school was on an assembly schedule, the second period was somewhat shorter than usual. The bell jingled indicating the beginning of the third period, my free period.

Before I could leave, the assistant Principal, Mr. Peninton came into the room.

"Could you cover room 207 for a while until we locate the substitute for that class?" He asked.

"Sure," I said. I wondered what had happened to the other substitute, had the students chased him or her out? I left and went to room 207.

"Hey, what kind of person are you?" A student asked as I came in. I didn't understand his question.

"Are you human or what?" He continued.

"Am I what?" I responded.

"Pardon this interruption. Will the substitute for room 207 please return to your room. Will the substitute for room 207 please return to your class. Thank you," the intercom crackled.

Before I could sit down, I saw the assistant principal in the hallway with a young lady. I presumed she was the substitute for this room.

"I was eating lunch, I'm sorry, I lost my schedule," the young lady gave one of the weakest excuses.

The assistant principal responded, "you have to be in your class this period. I'll send you another schedule up."

I looked at the young lady's face and saw signs of fatigue and stress, the kids must have been getting to her. I presumed she had taken an extended break and had gotten caught, that's all. I left and returned to my classroom. The clock showed ten minutes remaining in the third period. The fourth period began. Ten more minutes went by and no one showed. Then three girls came into the class, one was short and light, one medium in height, and the other a chubby, girl with short hair.

"Are you supposed to be in here this period?" I asked them.

"No. But can we stay in here until the bell rings?" One of them asked.

"I guess you can. So long as you don't start acting up."

"Thank you mister."

"How do you like Spinley?" A girl asked.

"It's kind of wild around here during this time of the year isn't it?" I answered

"Have you ever been over to Bangley?" another girl asked me.

"Yes, I have." I said.

"In the bathroom there, girls in there smoking that stuff and shooting that junk. I almost got beat up by a gang of girls over there, that's why I transferred to Spinley." The girl shifted in her seat.

I realized that I wasn't the only one having problems, some of the students seemed to be getting their share also. I contemplated for a moment, what was the school system coming to? Things had changed drastically in the short span of time I had been out of high school. I wondered how the students now learned anything. There was more disruption now than when I was going. What kind of society was it that allowed the education and discipline of its children go degenerate so badly?

Who's fault was it? For deteriorating buildings and lack of supplies, was the administration to blame? What about the lack of discipline? Were the parents to blame? Was society as a whole at fault.? In the new permissive society where anything goes and the 'do your own thing' mentality, was that the reason?

And what about me? Who was I to judge? I probably drank more wine and popped more pills than anyone. But I had problems, but so does everyone else. I'm sure there were some dedicated teachers in the system and some dedicated students too.

The trouble in the schools was just a symptom of the overall problems in the whole country. But what could I do about it? The fault originated in the home. I felt that I was just trying to hold on until the three o'clock bell. I wondered what the system would do without substitutes. Yet substitutes received more abuse and neglect in the system than any other group. I still felt a sense of pride that I was of some use to society, despite my own shortcomings. Substitutes were the thin red line that separated the school system from total chaos.

"You got a cigarette mister?" One of the girls asked me, snapping me out of my contemplation.

"You're not allowed to smoke in school." I answered. I had some but I wasn't going to give them any.

"What about a joint? You got a joint?"

"No. Is that all you people think about?" Who was I to talk? Even though I didn't smoke that much marijuana.

"What else is there to think about? I like to come to school high, it's more fun that way." The girl leaned forward in her chair.

"How are you going to learn anything?" I asked.

"That's how we learn, when we're high. I go to sleep in class if I'm not high."

I shook my head. I remembered defiantly going to one of my college classes half drunk. I felt so foolish that I didn't do it again. I didn't even know what drugs were back then.

The fourth period ended and my lunch period began. I stayed at my desk and opened up my brown bag and ate my lunch. After I finished, I picked up a pencil and paper and wrote a poem. I titled the poem 'Song of the Substitute Teacher.'

My sixth period class came in on time to my surprise. I passed out the ditto sheets to keep them occupied. The period went by without incident until five minutes before the bell. Then the whole class just got up and left.

After the bell, my seventh period class came in and took their seats. I passed out the remaining ditto sheets. I couldn't believe how quietly they worked on the sheets. I thought I would reward the class by letting them leave early before they decided to walk out like my sixth period had.

"You people want to leave early?" I asked.

The whole class expressed agreement, except one little boy. "You can't let us go before the bell rings." The little boy was being difficult.

"Be quiet Tommy. If the man wants to let us go early, let him." Another student responded.

Tommy got up. "I'm going to tell the principal," he left the room.

"You really think he'll tell the principal?" I asked. "No, you can let us go. He was just playing."

"All right, you people can go." At five minutes to three I put my coat on and started to leave. Before I could get out the classroom door, Tommy and the principal appeared in front of me.

"Where's your class Mr. Johnson?" The principal inquired.

"I let them go a little early."

"Who gave you the authority to let them go before three o'clock?" His voice boomed.

"I didn't see any harm in..." I was cut short.

"Don't you know the students aren't supposed to leave the building until three o'clock?" If the truant officer catches them, they and I will be in a lot of trouble." I thought for a moment, letting them out early had been a tactical error.

"I'm going to have to suspend you indefinitely Mr. Johnson, I'm sorry."

"Now wait a minute. Don't you think you're a little too hard on me?"

"You'll be notified in the mail as to the duration of your suspension. That's all Mr. Johnson." The principal turned and left the room. I felt my heart in my throat.

"You can take this job and stick it up your you know what!" I screamed down the hall. The principal looked back and shook his head. I was furious. I left the school after throwing the key in the trash. What would I do now? I was really in trouble. I caught the bus to the Purple Giraffe. I tried to wash the dishes but the manager knew something was wrong.

"What's wrong, Cornell?" The manager asked.

"I got suspended from my day job." I said dejectedly.

"Go over to the bar and get yourself a drink, it's on the house," he continued, "you can have the rest of the night off. I'll get Harry to finish up in the kitchen."

"Thanks Lou, I really appreciate it," I said as I took off my apron and sat down at the bar. I ordered a double scotch on the rocks, straight, with no chaser. I looked around at the tables and was surprised to see Gail, Matson's sister. I wondered what she was doing up here. I drank the scotch down in an effort to hold it together. I couldn't let her know what had happened. I ordered another drink and went over to where she was sitting.

Gail didn't look anything like her brother Matson. Matson was dark and ugly and bald. Gail was light-skinned, slender and had more of a personality than her brother. And she had a job, something Matson didn't want. Gail looked at me, displaying no emotion that I could tell at the moment.

"Hello Gail, what brings you to the Purple Giraffe?" I asked as I sat down, trying to sound cheerful even though I was suffering inside.

"I came to see you." She said as she poured her beer.

"See me, about what?"

"About you and Matson."

"What about us?" I took a big gulp of my drink.

"I know about the bet you two made. I don't want to see either of you get hurt. I care about my brother Cornell. But Matson is slick, you have to watch him. He can get pretty nasty at times. He's out on bond now. I guess you heard about him getting arrested?" She looked at me intensely. I wondered what kind of game she was playing.

"Matson and I came up together. Even though I'm a substitute teacher and he's a hustler, we're still homeboys. If I win the bet, I'm sure he'll pay me. If I loose, I'll pay him. What's the problem?" I stated, trying to sound credible.

"Cornell, Matson's moving up. He's being backed by the 'Big Boys' now. He'll be dealing in weight instead of nickel and dime bags. Matson will easily be able to clear a thousand dollars a week if he beats his charges. How are you going to compete with that? What does a teacher make in a year? Ten thousand dollars? Twelve thousand? And if you don't pay him off when the time comes, he'll come looking for you. What will you do then Cornell? I don't want you two to have a gun battle and somebody gets shot. It's not worth it."

I knew she was telling the truth. I swallowed hard.

"That's if he beats the charges. He won't be able to make anything if he's in jail."

"Matson's trial's not until March. It's December now Cornell. What do you think Matson will be doing in the meantime, watching TV?"

I shuddered at the prospects. I didn't even make ten thousand dollars a year, I was just a substitute at that. I would be lucky to clear four thousand at the rate I was going.

"I wouldn't worry, Gail. Like I said, if I win, he'll pay me. If I loose, I'll pay him."

"Be careful Cornell. Even though Matson is my brother, I don't like to see him mess over people. He might try to pull something on you, so you better watch out."

Before I could say anything else, I looked up and saw Karen coming through the door. She looked over at us, with fire in her eyes. I hoped she didn't get the wrong idea.

"So this is how you've been spending your evenings after school. Up here with this, this tramp! I don't see you doing any work you no good, good for nothing..." Karen cried as she opened her purse and reached for something inside. My heart stopped. I hoped she didn't have a gun.

"Wait a minute now..." Gail spoke up.

"Karen, you've got the wrong idea..." I said as I stood up.

Karen pulled out a switch blade and lunged for me. I side stepped and kicked the chair toward her. She lost her balance and fell over the table. Before she could get up, I took the knife out of her hand. The people in the bar stared at us. I looked up at Lou. He gave me a harsh look.

"Let me up, let me up!" Karen screamed. "I'll get you for this. I loved you Cornell. Why are you doing this to me?"

"Let me explain Karen. You don't understand." I pleaded with her, but it was no good. Her mind was made up to see things the way she wanted to see them. I let her back up and backed away, wondering if she would go for me again with her fingernails.

"I'm leaving. When you get back home, I'll be gone. I hope you and this, this... I hope you'll be happy. I'll never forget this." Karen stormed out of the bar. My mouth hung wide open.

"I'm sorry Cornell. I didn't know your woman was so jealous. I'll go and explain everything to her." Gail tried to comfort me.

"That's all right Gail. I'll take care of it. Once I get home and talk to her, she'll understand it was all a misunderstanding."

I walked toward Lou to apologize for what had happened, but it didn't do any good. He told me he couldn't have that type of trouble at his restaurant, it was bad for business. He wrote me out a check and told me not to come back. I left the Purple Giraffe, barely holding back the tears. I tried to get back home before Karen left. It seemed that my whole life was coming apart. Maybe I should have married Karen. Then she might not have been so quick to leave. I just didn't believe in marriage. I was soon coming to the point of not believing much in anything anymore. What was the point, nothing seemed to be working out.

10. Song of the Substitute Teacher

Who comes in to hold the line?

When our schools go in decline?

The Substitute Teacher.

Who is a walking target

For <u>all</u> the students to upset?

Who loves the students

More than their parents?

In order to put up with their antics?

The Substitute Teacher.

Who's the first to be cursed

And the last to be praised?

For all his patience

On stormy Mondays?

Who takes more abuse

Than old mother goose?

Ducking erasers and pencils

And books and refuse?

Three cheers for the Substitute Teacher.

No tears for the Substitute Teacher.

Our kids love the Substitute Teacher.

Our schools need the Substitute Teacher.

11. Twilight Zone

It had been a bleak Christmas for me that winter. I thought all the powers that be had conspired against me. I had lost two jobs and my woman, all in one day, and the bet was still on.

I would not forget that night. I came back to the apartment and vainly tried to persuade Karen not to leave. She was too stubborn to listen, and she left. I looked around the apartment and missed the presence of female companionship. I had to do all the chores myself now.

It was February, and I still hadn't received a letter in the mail from the school system letting me know when I could come back to work. It wouldn't matter, in another week, the phone would be cut off and I wouldn't be able to call in anyway. I was living off what little I had saved up. Now I was down almost to my last penny. I poured another glass of 'King Rose Wine' and continued to feel sorry for myself. I figured it was just a matter of time. I was behind in the rent again. I couldn't borrow anymore money from anybody, because there was no way I could repay them. I had worked down at the corner store for a while, but had to quit, when the manager smelled wine on my breath one day.

Most of the time I sat by the window and looked out for the mailman. Hoping he would bring me some word from the school system that I could come back to work before they cut my phone off. I didn't go out much anymore, I just sat in my apartment and cried to myself, wondering if I would ever get straight again.

Before I could pour myself another drink, I heard someone knocking at the door. I jumped up. It couldn't be the mailman, it was too early. I put the thought out of my mind that it might be Karen. I went to the door and looked out of the peep hole. It was Gail. I didn't want to be bothered with her again, she was the reason Karen had left. Finally Gail got tired of knocking. I looked out the window and saw her walk down the street. I finished pouring another glass of 'King Rose' and continued to sit by the window.

I could see the kids on their way to school and that brought back better memories. I looked out at the lucky people who were on their way to work. I wished like everything that I could have been out there with them this morning on my way to work. I sipped some wine and saw Matson's Cadillac ease down the street in front of my third floor apartment. Abruptly he pulled over to the curb and it looked like he was talking to Bug and Blackjack. I saw Blackjack exchange money for a small bit of aluminum foil. I knew what was happening. The aluminum foil reflected the morning sun up to me. I knew that the dope was in the foil.

I thought about turning in Matson, but I couldn't bring myself to do it. Not just because we had come up together. I still held on to the outmoded belief of honoring bets made fair and square. I figured that now I was paying for my honesty.

At least no one would be able to accuse me of being a snitch. And that wasn't my style anyway. May the best man win fair and square was my motto. I wondered if those would be my last words.

How did this happen to me? After four years of hard labor to capture a liberal arts degree, I came to the dismal realization that a bachelor's degree didn't seem to be enough. Maybe I needed a master's degree or Ph. D? But that cost money. I needed a full time job. But getting one seemed to elude my grasp. I went into the bedroom and laid down for a short nap.

I was awakened by a knock at the door.

"Who is it?" I asked.

"My name is George Hampton and I'm from the Shekinah Baptist Church. We're in the neighborhood passing out tracts and telling people about salvation through Jesus Christ. Would you like to know more about salvation?"

"Why not, come in," I said. What did I have to loose? And maybe I might be able to get some money from them if I played my cards right. And there goes that word again, 'salvation'. Maybe I needed to find out more about this so-called salvation.

George came in accompanied with another young lady, who looked to be in her early twenties. They both sat down on my couch and opened their bibles. What a bunch of religious fanatics. I pulled up a chair directly across from them.

"Are you people for real? I mean no one really believes in the bible. If anyone did, the world wouldn't be the way it is. There are nothing but hypocrites, women, children and homosexuals in the churches. The churches aren't helping the world. Just look at the way things are in the world." I let out all of my frustrations on them.

"Let me show you something," George continued as he flipped the pages of his bible. "According to John 3:16, for God so loved the world, that he gave his only begotten Son, that whosoever believeth in him should not perish, but have everlasting life."

The young lady spoke up. "Also in the book of Romans, chapter 6, verse 23, for the wages of sin is death, but the gift of God is eternal life through Jesus Christ our Lord."

George looked at me. "Even though the whole world is in a bad situation, there is a way out, and that's through Jesus Christ. If we repent and turn away from our sins and accept the sacrifice he made for us on Calvary, we can be saved from going to hell. Don't you want to be saved, Mr., Mr. ,"

"Johnson," I stuttered, "Cornell Johnson. I believe you make your own heaven and hell right here on this earth. I don't believe in any pie-in-the-sky religion."

"Mr. Johnson."

"Yeah."

"What type of work do you do?" George asked.

"I am, or was a substitute teacher for the city school system."

"Do you like your work?" George asked.

"Not really. It's nothing but a blackboard jungle in the schools. The kids act like maniacs and no one seems to care," I responded.

"Did you ever wonder why it's like that?"

"Yeah I wonder why? Why is it like that."

George paused for a moment, and flicked through his bible again. "In Proverbs, chapter 22, verse 6, it says to train up a child in the way he should go: and when he is old, he will not depart from it. If people would bring their children up according to the way the bible says they should, we wouldn't have the problems we have in the schools and homes."

I wondered if he was right. George and the young lady closed their bibles and stood up. "We enjoyed talking to you Mr. Johnson, here's something you can read in your spare time." They handed me some religious tracts.

"Before we leave Mr. Johnson, can we pray for you?" George asked.

"Sure, why not." I said. What did I have to loose? Who knows, maybe there might be something to this Christian religion. I probably needed somebody to pray for me. All that I was going through.

"Dear Father God, we come before you right now praying for our dear brother Cornell. You know what he has need of, we don't know the problem. We are asking that you set him free from anything that is hindering him, heal his body of any sickness or disease, allow him to be prosperous and be saved. In Jesus' name, amen." George finished.

"By the way, do you have a few dollars I can get from you?" I inquired.

"Sure, here's a few dollars." George handed me a few dollars. He and the lady then left.

I looked at the empty 'King Rose' wine bottles, time for a refill. I went to the refrigerator and looked for another. There were none. I checked my supply of pills, just two left. Ever since I left high school I'd been drinking wine and liquor. It was only recently that I started into pills. It seemed to be a 'rite of manhood' in the neighborhood where I grew up. If you couldn't drink at least a pint of wine straight down, you were considered some kind of sissy or something.

I looked on top of the table and counted my change. Maybe that was my problem, the wine and the pills. It was strange, for the first time I thought about trying to stop drinking and popping pills. Cold turkey, I knew it would be rough, but I had to at least try. I threw the empty bottle of 'King Rose' into the trash can. It clanked against several other empty bottles. It would be a while before the mail came. I tossed the rest of the pills down the toilet and laid down on the bed. I tried to sleep but my thoughts were disjointed. After tossing and turning, I finally settled for gazing up at the ceiling for the time being. Time seemed to be slowing down at a torturous pace.

I closed my eyes and all kinds of visions flashed into view. Fiery, violent, furious...fade away, indignation, Matson's bald head aglow.

Inexorable unrelenting mercilessness, purple giraffes danced around a vengeful image of Karen. Secluded moods burst modestly between classrooms and bathrooms. Fugue, out of control, mind flight. fade away, keen emotion flooded my senses.

     My mind ebbed and flowed, then I drifted off into a feverish sleep. When I awoke, I didn't know how long I'd been sleep. I glanced over at the clock, nine o'clock. I wondered if it was day or night. I couldn't understand why I'd slept so long. I felt myself wet all over, I was sweating. I got up to eat something, my appetite was returning. I reached into the refrigerator for some day-old beans and put them on the stove to heat up. The aroma filtered through the apartment. There was nothing like the smell of red beans and rice. I poured some into a bowl and sat down for breakfast. No sooner had they hit my stomach when everything came back up.

     I cleaned the vomit off the floor. As I swept it in the trash, I started to shake. First my hands started shaking, then my arms, until my whole body was shaking. I got back in bed and just laid there, shaking. I shook for a good two hours until it finally subsided somewhat. I wondered how long I would have to go through this. I got up to drink some water. I was surprised when it didn't come back up. Back to bed I went for some rest. Somehow, I drifted off to sleep.

     I had lost track of time. Another day had slipped away and my mind seemed to be slipping away at a faster pace. I got up and my legs almost gave way. My stomach was still upset and now I began to ache all over. I went to the medicine cabinet for some aspirins and antacid, but all of that came back up in the sink. I knew I would have to ride this one out without too much help from any more pills. I looked out the window and saw the sun filtering its rays through the blinds for the second time in a row. I groped for the radio and turned it on. The music was painful to my ears but I wanted to find out what day it was.

     "...the boss sound in this here town. This is Hot Poppa coming' at you on this here first day of March, playing the best sounds in this here town..."

I clicked the radio off. The last thing I remembered after pouring my last glass of King Rose was that it was the twenty second of February. Now it was March first. I thought only three days had gone by since then. But according to the man on the radio, six days had elapsed. There were three days unaccounted for in my memory.

While I was trying to sort out the missing days in my memory, I heard another knock at my door.

"Who is it?" Would I ever be able to get any rest?

"Blackjack, it's Blackjack."

I opened the door and saw that Blackjack was not alone. He was with Janice, the neighborhood 'Wild Child', and her hair was sticking straight up. She would be a pretty nice looking girl if she could do something about her hair. No doubt she hadn't had time to comb it from previous night's escapades.

"I'm glad you're home Cornell," Blackjack said as they came in.

"What you been doing for it? We thought we'd stop by and say hello. I got some wine too. Where you been hiding? I haven't seen you for a while."

"I haven't been feeling well." I continued. "I think I might have the flu or something."

"Yeah, it is getting kind of nippy out there," Blackjack drawled as he glanced over at Janice. "Look here, " Blackjack pulled me over to the side so Janice couldn't hear what he was saying. "Can me and Janice have a little party at your crib?"

I thought about it for a moment, what the heck. I could use some company.

"Yeah, you can use my bedroom. I don't want my bed messed up, you know how it is. It takes me so long to get around to washing my sheets, since Karen's been gone." I finished whispering back to Blackjack.

"Solid," Blackjack whispered back.

"I'm sorry about you and Karen." Blackjack tried to sound concerned.

I didn't even want to say anything.

Blackjack pulled a fifth of wine out of a brown paper bag and set it on the table. "Here's some wine for you partner, just save me a hit," he smiled. He then pulled Janice's arm as they both went into my bedroom.

I sat at the table staring at the wine, fighting down the urge to pour myself a drink. What a temptation. I had been on the wagon for six days. I held my hand out, I still had the shakes. But I fought it, with every ounce of will power I could summon. I was determined not to take a drink. I was not going to drink anymore wine, not today, not tomorrow, not ever again. If I could hold out a little longer, maybe I could get through this.

I could hear Janice's and Blackjack's laughter echoing from the bedroom. But strangely, I didn't feel the slightest urge to join them. Not because Karen was gone, but because my body still ached something terrible. I had difficulty just moving around. I knew I wouldn't be in any shape for much of anything.

Abruptly Blackjack bopped out of the room, looking like a kid who just ate a whole quart of his favorite ice cream.

"I got to run down the street for a minute Cornell. I'll be right back." He glanced over at the unopened bottle of wine. "You must really be sick," he chuckled, "that's the first time I've seen you not take a drink when it was right in front of you."

"Yeah, I guess I am sick," I told the truth this time. The sickness I had was not the sickness he thought. Blackjack went out the door.

"Cornell, Cornell," I heard Janice's voice from the bedroom. I made my way to the bedroom, still shaking, and peeped in the door. Janice looked at me, "Come here, baby." She sounded so sweet. My body felt like someone had been using it as a punching bag. I was in no shape for any romance. My back was stiff, I could hardly bend over.

"I'm not feeling well Janice, sorry," I sounded pitiful. I turned around to go back into the living room.

"Nigga you must be sick!" I heard her scream behind my back.

I sat back down and looked at the unopened bottle of wine. I could have used a drink right now, but I fought it, no, not this time. No, not this time, or anymore times. I had to fight it. I wasn't going to let it beat me. I stared at the bottle. How long, how long would my withdrawal last, how long? I was cowering at the notion of it lasting even another minute.

Janice stormed out the bedroom and then out the door without saying a word. All I saw was a blur of her red coat, that's how fast she was moving and how disorientated I was. It didn't even look like she had a dress on under her coat. Twenty minutes later, Blackjack came back.

"Where's Janice?" He asked.

"She left."

"What did you do to her?'

"Nothing, I didn't do anything to her. I think that was the problem." Blackjack looked at me strangely and then scooped up the bottle and put it back in the brown bag.

"I guess I'll split now. You look like you really don't feel too good. You better get some rest. See you later," Blackjack said and went out the door. I didn't say anything. I just stared off into space like a man in a trance.

Tired and fatigued, I felt my thoughts starting to skip again. To hold on to a remnant of rationality, I took out a pencil and piece of paper and began to write another poem. I scribbled the title on the page: 'Ode To King Rose.'

After writing a few stanzas, I wandered into the bedroom and flopped down on the mattress. I closed my eyes and saw colors dissolve and then reintegrate themselves. There was a ringing in my ears as my consciousness expanded, then swelled, and then I floated off into a lethargic slumber.

12. Ode to King Rose

Where is my wine?
My 'King Rose Wine'?
I've got to ease my mind,
One more time.

Well now, one dollar
Will get me a bottle,
Now I'll hoop and holler,
Slip and totter.

One sip,
And I'll do a flip,
One quart,
And I'll tear you apart.

There's nothing more potent,
Than some 'King Rose Wine',
It makes me feel confident,
It makes me feel fine.

Now the bottle is empty,
And my hands start to shake,
I see old Mr. D.T.,
My mind. he is about to take.

13. Teacher Strike

I felt strong enough to go to the store to pick up a newspaper. It was a brisk March day, the wind blew the leaves on the trees. The sun darted in and out of the clouds. I overcome my paranoia and left the apartment. I still felt I was still walking in a daze.

The bold letters of the headlines caught my bloodshot eyes: <u>Teachers On Strike.</u> The words jolted me like an electric shock. Instantly I felt like a sleepwalker that had been rudely awakened. Slowly, my thought patterns reorganized themselves into a coherent sequence. I then realized I hadn't checked my mailbox in several days.

I ran up the street back to my apartment. A little boy looked at me as if I were a long distance runner. I got to my mailbox after outrunning a stray dog on the way and flipped open the lock with my key. Inside, several days mail were crammed together. I thumbed frantically through the letters until I came across a school system letter postmarked last week. I opened it and read that my suspension had ended and I could come back to work. I could have been back to work last week if only I had checked my mailbox. I thought twice. I might not have been in any shape to work last week, I was still recovering from cold turkey. Ready or not, I was going back to work. I had to get out of my apartment before I went stir crazy.

I called the phone company and asked them to extend the due date on my bill, they complied to my relief. After receiving an assignment, I settled down for the rest of the day in strong anticipation for the next day's adventure.

Goulden Junior High was one of those schools where you could easily get lost. Its winding corridors and recessed classrooms formed a small maze that only the teachers and students were familiar with. I had difficulty finding my classroom. With the help of a student, I finally located it and walked into the room after unlocking the door.

All of the classrooms were starting to look the same. There wasn't much that could be done in the way of variety with wooden desks and chairs. I was surprised that I didn't have to cross a picket line and reasoned it probably was for the better.

I had a total of three students in my homeroom. Most parents were keeping the children home during the strike. In a way I was glad there was a strike. The less students I had to deal with, the better. Even with the small attendance, the administration was hard pressed in keeping the schools open in the wake of the strike. A few teachers had come in, those who were not in the union. Other than that, the classrooms would be manned by substitutes or no one at all. I knew the students who did show up would have a field day.

Being inside a classroom again was helping me feel like my <u>old self.</u> My withdrawal symptoms and paranoia were dissipating. My feeling of being useful again was helping me to overcome.

"Good morning," the words came over the intercom, "today is Friday, March twenty-ninth, 1974. Due to reduced personnel because of the teacher's strike, we will have a short assembly today explaining our procedures in this emergency."

The bell rang and I accompanied my three students to the auditorium. The principal gave us a short pep talk on the do's and don'ts for the present situation. I tried to keep from falling asleep. It was finally over and I returned to my room.

The Substitute Teacher: Baptism of Fire

Today was the first day I had went to school without the help of any pills. I felt so much better. For the first time in a long time I was optimistic. The turmoil of the previous months was fading from my memory like a bad dream.

I felt more alive and exuberant. I felt as if I could run around the block three times without getting tired. I was not bitter now about the previous months, I felt stronger because of it. Maybe in a way it was a good thing I had been through the fire. It caused me to discard some bad habits that had been giving me nothing but problems.

I had one student in my first period. He had his coat on and his hat, as if he was about to go home at any moment.

"Hi," he said as he sat down.

"Hi, are you the only one to show up for this class?"

"No, the rest of the class either went home or are walking the halls," the boy replied.

"This strike is causing some disruption." I glanced at the morning paper I had brought. The boy sat at his desk quietly for the rest of the period. We were on a special schedule so the bell rang early. My second period was my free period, but I had been instructed to cover another room because of the shortage of personnel.

I walked in to room 115 and sat down. Twenty minutes went by and no one showed. I took out the paper and continued reading, looking up occasionally at the door. These were the type of days I liked. I hoped the strike would continue.

The second period bell chimed and I went to the lounge for my lunch break. The lounge empty. I walked over to the table and saw some 'Strike' pamphlets. I picked one up and read it. It was evident to me that the complaint procedure had broken down. Not only were the schools in disarray, but teachers-administration relations must have been strained to the breaking point. I looked at another pamphlet and gaped in disbelief at the proposed budget cuts:

Elimination of 1500 teaching jobs to save $15,000,000

Reduction of heat and lights costs to save $200,000

Termination of adult education classes to save $7,000,000

Elimination of substitute teachers to save $3,000,000

Elimination of special education school to save $1,000,000

Reduction of building maintenance to save $4,800,000

"Pardon this interruption, at the ringing of the bell, the school will close early today because of the strike. All substitute teachers are asked to call in for their assignments. The schools will be open next week on a limited basis until the strike is resolved. Thank you." The voice on the intercom sounded tired and strained.

The bell sounded and I left the room after picking up a copy of 'The Educator'. It hadn't occurred to me that they might have to close the schools until the strike was over or that they were trying to do away with substitutes all together. Now I realized that the strike wasn't such a good thing after all.

I got on the bus and crossed my fingers and hoped that somehow the teachers and administration would put their heads together to end the walkout. I glanced through an article in 'The Educator', as I rode the bus home:

'The average student and teacher has 1 chance in 9 of being a victim of theft, 1 chance in 80 of being attacked, and 1 chance in 200 of being robbed. Furthermore, 50% of all assaults of 12 to 15 year olds occur in schools, and 68% of robberies. Heroin is available to 14% of students attending the city school, available to 11% who attend small city schools, 9% attending suburban schools and 8% for rural schools. One large city school system reported 11,380 incidents of arson, fire, and thefts alone with 2,400 incidents of assaults. But only 1/3 of all incidents are reported to the police.'

14. Day Two, Rosemont Elem. School

The teacher strike was finally over. My first day at Rosemont was perfect. I looked forward to my second day. I walked up the steps and entered the building. Rosemont was a modern school by most standards, and it was something to look at too. It was built on the site of the old elementary school I attended as a kid. Now the new Rosemont and old had nothing in common except the name.

Through the grapevine I heard that Matson was given a year probation on his charges. I also heard that Matson was starting to use his own stuff and was fast becoming his own 'best customer'. In a way I felt sorry for him and in another way I hoped he was his own 'best customer'. If he used more than he could sell, I still might have a chance to win the bet. But if that was to be the situation, I doubt if Matson would be able to pay me and the monkey on his back.

I would then be faced with the <u>neighborhood</u> <u>imperative</u> of doing something to him. If I didn't, but just let it slide, I wouldn't be able to show my face on the street.

It seemed that either way, I would be a loser. After signing in, I went to the classroom, where my sixth graders were. Before I could pass out the student's work, I saw the principal, Mr. Harris and a woman come in the door. Mr. Harris was expressionless but the woman had an evil look on her face.

"My little girl came home yesterday and said you were drawing pictures of naked women on the blackboard. Is this true?" The woman demanded. I thought back to what I did yesterday.

"No, it is not true. I didn't draw any naked women on the blackboard. I drew some stick people on the board when I was trying to explain a question. I don't know why your little girl thought I was drawing naked people." These kids have vivid imaginations, I told myself.

"All right, I don't know why she would tell me something like that." The woman looked at me intensely.

"I don't know either," I said calmly, wishing the woman would leave. The woman, with an unconvinced look on her face, left the room with Mr. Harris. I continued to pass out the work and overheard some students talking about a T.V. program they saw last night.

"Yeah, that man came in the window and got that lady. He made her take all her clothes off and then he put a knife to her neck and made her do it with him. Did you see it on T.V. Johnny?" A boy asked.

"Uh huh, I saw it."

"Hey," I interrupted their conversation, "you two turn around and start on your work.." I handed them some ditto sheets and folders. I pondered the effect of such television programs on sixth grade students. I left the building at twelve noon and took an extended lunch break after escorting my class to the cafeteria.

When I returned, I could tell by the students' faces something was wrong.

"What's wrong?" I asked one of the students.

"Stephanie's crying." Another student answered mischievously.

"What happened?" I asked as I entered the room and saw Stephanie crying.

"What's wrong Stephanie? Why are you crying?" I asked as I took a paper napkin out and dried her eyes. Stephanie didn't answer me. She just looked at me with tear-soaked eyes and continued sobbing.

"Will somebody please tell me what happened."

"Mr. Johnson, some boys dragged Stephanie into the bathroom during the lunch period and stuck their things in her and held her down."

Their answer put me in a state of paralysis. Stephanie couldn't have been more than 12 years old. And the boys no older than 13. The disturbing truth became apparent. Stephanie had been raped.

"I want everyone to come down to the office with Stephanie and me. Someone is going to tell the principal what happened while I was gone." I barked in disgust.

I took Stephanie and the class down to the office and told the principal what had happened.

"Can you tell us who the boys were who did this to you?" The principal asked Stephanie as I looked on in uncertainty.

Stephanie shook her head in agreement and pointed to the same boys in the class who had been discussing the T.V. program. It was startling to realize that what the boys had seen on T.V, they had tried to duplicate in school.

"Where were you when all of this happened?" The principal asked me as he pushed the boys into another room.

"I was on my lunch break," I answered defensively.

"Why didn't you lock the door when you left?" The principal asked.

"You didn't give me a key," I answered.

I left the office and returned to my classroom in an agitated state. I glanced out of the window and saw three police cars pull up. I left my class and went to find out what was going on. Near the end of the corridor I could see a crowd of students and teachers, and then I heard the shrill voice of Stephanie's mother.

"What kind of principal are you to let something like this happen to my child!"

A scuffle followed as I saw Stephanie's mother hit the principal with a baseball bat. He crumpled to the floor as the police grabbed the hysterical woman and pulled her away. Someone took the principal to the hospital. At three o'clock I left the school wondering what would happen next.

15. Day One, Horrible Hammond

I was relieved to receive a junior high assignment, Rosemont had been one trying experience. Hammond Junior High was a moderately old school, with a few broken windows and walls of graffiti. Above the door were written the words, 'Horrible Hammond'. Security was tight, with bolts and special locks on the doors.

"Rinnnngggggg." The first period bell echoed throughout the building.

"Can we give our book reports today? A girl asked

"No, wait until your teacher comes back." I said.

"Can we act out a play in class?"

"No, you better wait until your teacher comes back." I repeated. A boy came in running through the door. After he sat down, I looked at him.

"Are you supposed to be in here?" Before he could answer, a teacher burst into the door.

"Hey boy, come here!" the teacher yelled. The boy just sat there. The teacher, a dark complexioned young lady, moved toward him quickly.

"I told you to come here boy! What the hell do you think this is? I'm a lady. You better show me some respect!" The teacher grabbed the boy by his shirt and pulled him out of the class.

I told myself things were getting off to a very good start this morning. I was able to cope with incidents such as those better now. The ability to keep a clear head gave me more confidence in dealing with the students' pranks.

The second period bell sounded. As I looked down the hallway at the passing students, I saw one boy pick a girl up by the waist and carry her down the hall as if he were carrying a bag of potatoes.

I looked across the hall to the room opposite mine and noticed a female student yelling into the room. The girl would yell and them run down the hall, come back, and yell again and run down the hall again. This went on for several minutes until the teacher, a large woman, had gotten enough. She ran out the room after the girl. The girl stopped and turned and they squared off, looking like they were about to fight each other. I stepped between them. I told the female student to go to her class. The teacher criticized me for not letting them fight to my surprise. Afterwards, I regretted not letting them fight.

I returned to my class and took a seat behind the desk.

"Will you be here tomorrow, Mr?" Asked a student.

"I don't know. The way things are going, who can tell?" I answered.

"Well, if you do come back tomorrow," a girl continued, "we'll have a surprise for you."

I wondered what kind of surprise she was talking about. I looked around on the desk to see if the teacher had left an English assignment, but didn't find any. I then formulated my own assignment for the students.

"I want you people to take out a pen and piece of paper. I want you to write me a one-page essay on what you did over the weekend."

Some of the students grumbled about the assignment but most of them worked on the essay diligently and turned their paper in before the bell rang. .

"Rinnnggg." The third period bell chimed. I stepped outside of the classroom to supervise the students passing through the halls. My third period class took their seats. Before I returned to my desk, I saw some other students loitering outside the door. I went toward them.

"All right, let's clear the halls, let's clear the halls. You people should go to your third period class," I said.

Suddenly, a tall boy pulled out what looked like a gun. It may have been a toy gun. He pointed it at me.

"You can't tell me what to do. I ought to shoot you now. Why don't you clear the hall." The boy growled.

I wasn't about to argue with him. I didn't know whether or not the gun was real. I wasn't taking any chances. I dashed back into the classroom and bolted the door and put both locks on. Now I realized why they had so many locks on the doors.

At this point, I longed for some tranquilizers. I trembled as I pressed the call buzzer.

"Yes," was the response over the intercom.

"Could you send security to room 222. A student may have a gun outside of my classroom. I don't know if it is real or not."

"All right. We will send someone," the voice came back cool and businesslike.

A few minutes later, security arrived in my classroom.

"Whoever it was, they are gone now," the security person informed me.

"We will do a sweep of the school and check students that are in the hallway," the security person stated and then left.

"I want you people to take out a piece of paper and pen and write a one-page essay about what you did over the weekend." I wanted to get the class working so I could calm down. The students complied, I flinched at every unseen sound. I continued to look toward the door and was fearful about going back into the hallway.

The fourth period bell clanged. It was my lunch period. I looked timidly up and down the halls before I walked quickly to the teachers' lounge. My fears subsided somewhat as I took a seat across from some other teachers. I leaned back and was in disbelief at their display of normality.

"Some girl students dragged a boy in the girls' bathroom last week and molested him. I think we should put locks on the bathrooms, to keep something like that from happening again." A middle aged male teacher entertained the idea of increased security for the bathrooms.

"What is to be done about some students extorting money from other students?" Another teacher posed the question. A detached silence hung over the lounge.

"I don't know about anyone else but I'm hungry. Who's going to join me in the cafeteria?" The middle aged man said.

The rest of the teachers nodded in agreement and left the lounge with him. I nibbled on a candy bar I had brought as a snack. Despite the day's confrontation, I congratulated myself for feeling more fit to deal with the students with a clear head. I enjoyed substituting more now. And the students didn't seem to be as aggravating as they had been when I was taking the pills.

A few minutes later, two more teachers entered the lounge, one young man and one young woman.

"How are you today?" The young man squeaked in a high-pitched voice. I tried to ignore it at first, but it continued to irritate me.

"I'm fine and you?" I answered.

"Are you subbing today?" The woman spoke up.

"Yes, I am."

The woman turned to the young man and they began to talk after they were seated.

"I'm glad you're back David. You were out for a while weren't you? What happened?" The woman asked the young man.

"I've been in the hospital. I had all kinds of things wrong with me girl. I had a heart attack, and I had an operation on my rectum. I almost spent a whole year in the hospital recuperating."

"You're too young to be having heart attacks," the young woman gave her opinion.

I listened to them intently. They had some strange characters at this school.

"That's what I thought too," The young man chuckled.

"That reminds me of a bad year I had a few years back." The woman continued. "It began when I fell down the steps at the senior prom. Soon after someone ran into my car. It was a total loss. To top it off, that was the same year I had to have surgery."

The bell clanged indicating the beginning of the fifth period. I returned to my classroom. I again instructed my fifth period class to write a one-page essay on what they did over the weekend. I noticed that some students weren't working on the assignment. I walked over toward them to see what they were doing. One student was tossing pieces of paper into the trashcan as if he were playing basketball.

Another was drawing dirty pictures on paper. Another girl was writing different zodiac signs on her notebook. I looked over to the other side of the room and saw a girl platting another girl's hair. One boy got up and started turning around in circles. He then sat back down as if nothing had happened.

I cautioned the students to do their work and to stop goofing off. At the end of the day I collected all the papers and took them with me to correct. After I got home, I changed into more comfortable clothes and settled down for a long evening correcting the student's papers:

Annette Clark Section 9-12 April, 1974 Period II

(English)
What I did over the week end. I went outside and played.
I helped my mother cooked dinner. I went over my grandmother house.

George Smith 4/74
English
Period II
Essay
All I did this weekend was play basketball in the Gym. And I went and played outside.

My Weekend
First of all I would like to say I had fun just being home. I got ripped and tripped out off of my cousin. Then we went out and on Sunday I slept until 4:30 P.M.
Thank You Wilhelmina Harris April, 1974

Beverly Loomis 9-12 April, 1974
Period II
English Essay

Over the weekend I found a lot to do. I made a german chocolate cake topped with ice cream. I found it hard to keep my family out of it. Then I went to party on Saxon Avenue, and had a ball with my friends. You know, you think you can trust people but you found out you can't. At the party my best friends jacket was stolen-. We all started making noise, and I started fussing like it was mine. They put me and my friends out of the party. I told them to kiss what I twist. Sunday I looked at a movie on T.V. The Incredible Shrinking Man. About a man who kept getting smaller and smaller. I was sleep most of the day, and when I did wake up I talked on the phone to my friend Loddy. I told her, "Loddy you should not mess around with marijuana. It could mess up you system." She told me that she only tried it one time, I said, "Once is enough!!!"

Gerald Johnson

I had a wonderful weekend!!

On Friday I went to a party in it was a very nice party, They had beer & wine and food. On Saturday I went to the movie and lots of fun. After we left from the movies, we went to the Disco party. On sunday I stay in the house in whatch television all day long.

Darryl Brodey

April, 1974

What I did over the weekend

I really didn't do anything much but go to the store go over my friends house go over girl houses and just walk around

Terry Bevins 9-12

I went home and broke my thumb, cut my knee and got bit by a dog. After all of that, I went roller skating. Later I met up with my cousin and we went to the best party in the world. After the party it was around 3 or 4 o'clock in the morning

Daniel Walker

April, 1974

Period III

What i did on the weekend i stayed in the house and watch television and slept and went to the store.

Edward Campbell

I was in bed all weekend long I got to eat and went to bed. and girl came to visit me. and I was just in bed.

Janice Young April, 1974 Period 3

I was looking at T.V. The Attack of the Dog People then when that went off a got on the phone the next day I went visiting thats all I can tell you. The End

Kathleen Singleton April, 1974

Period 3 Section 8-14 English

I stayed in the house all weekend. What I did was clean up a little bit, watch television, played records, and listen to the radio most of the time.

Darlene Latimrer

Ms. Corey   April, 1974

room--207   6th Period

English

Friday I didn't go to school because it was too cold. I went over Mamie's house later that evening, and at night I went blind. Saturday I went to a party and I was, hey I can't really say.

Sunday I did my history homework and study my english. I was sick all night.

Charlene Mason Period 6

English

During the weekend I was watching T.V. and drawing pictures. I went over my aunt's house help her fit a puzzle.

Sunday to church and sang. Then I went back to a 6:00 service. Praise the Lord! Praise Jesus Christ for saving me!

    I finally gave up trying to correct the papers in detail. The spelling and grammar was too disjointed for me to really grade correctly. I decided to either mark them 'Satisfactory' or 'Unsatisfactorily'. By giving the students the essay assignment I thought I could gain insight as to how their minds worked, but it only increased my confusion. I had formed my own theory on how to best handle the kids at school. It helped if I had my personal life together. The less worries outside of the classroom I had, the better I could function in the class.

    I had to be careful to not get in the position of fighting against the whole class. This situation would always bring too much animosity from the whole class and not just the trouble makers. The trick was to concentrate on the trouble makers.

    I found that if I reduced the number of hours I stayed up late going to parties or movies, that helped. Getting enough sleep was a necessity. The students would pounce on even a regular teacher if they sensed that the teacher was tired or 'out of it,' and more so for a substitute.

    On top of the list of priorities would be to try to maintain my 'cool' at all times as long as possible. When trouble-making students found that I didn't get upset easily, they usually discontinued their probing. Failing in maintaining my 'cool, the next best tactic was to be strict. I had to draw a line and let the students know that if they crossed it, they would be in trouble.

Another technique that kept disruption down to a minimum was to make sure the students had some work to do. Even though all the students didn't do the work, it was better to have some work for them than none at all. A mistake to avoid was trying to enforce absolute silence. I would let them talk as long as they didn't get too noisy.

I tried to maintain my cool most of the time if possible. Being tense and nervous just didn't work. Generally the students typed substitutes into three catergories, nice, mean, and trip. I was nice if I let them do what they wanted to do, mean if I didn't, and a trip if I did the unexpected. I tried to roll with the punches by either reacting positively, negatively or unexpectedly to any student disruptions or antics.

The teachers had the advantage of being able to grade and get to know the students. A substitute had very little in the way of grading students even for misconduct. And everyday was a new situation. I would have to learn how to handle the unexpected.

Most of all I found that if I showed them a little concern I could get things done. But if I hated them, I usually had to pay dearly for that state of mind.

After checking the papers, I put them into my briefcase and settled back in bed for a restful sleep. But I couldn't get any. All I could think about was Karen. I thought I'd forgotten about her, but I was wrong. I hadn't even gone out with another woman. Maybe that's what I needed to take my mind off of her, another woman.

I wanted to submerge myself in subbing, but it didn't seem to be working. I didn't get to sleep until about 4:00 A.M., and by then it was time for me to get back up.

16. Day Two, Horrible Hammond

I didn't know what to expect on my second day at Hammond. I kept thinking about what a girl in my second period had said yesterday, that they would have a surprise for me. I unlocked the door, but before I could step in to the room, I heard some cursing across the hall. I looked back and saw a short, large-lipped little boy, who couldn't have been more than three and a half feet tall calling a six foot tall, heavy-set woman teacher all kinds of names.

"You grit-colored pee-pot looking witch! You can't tell me what to do!" the boy continued, his coat draped over his arm as if he were concealing something.

"Who are you talking to boy? Don't you know I'll slap your face in!" The teacher screamed back at him. She lunged toward him in an attempt to grab him by the neck but the boy was too fast. In a twinkling he ducked and ran down the hall, steadily cursing the teacher.

"They're starting off early this morning," I sympathized with the woman teacher.

"These kids are something, aren't they?" She said as she went into her room. I nodded in agreement and went into my room. I took my coat off and sat down, expecting another 'crazy' day. I took the attendance and read the morning announcements. I glanced up at the blackboard and saw that someone had thoughtfully written some do's and don'ts:

DO'S:

(1) Write on the desks
(2) Leave paper in the desks
Curse one another out
Fight the teachers
Write on the wall
Hook classes
Pop gum as loudly as possible

DON'TS:

Don't come to school at 9:00, come when you feel like it
Don't come to school without candy
Don't go to class, if you do, go to sleep
Don't listen to teachers
Don't do your homework
      by the Do's and Don'ts

This was a sad state of affairs that some students thought it was fun to come to school and not learn.

"We are on regular schedule today. There will be a PTA meeting tomorrow night at 7:30. All parents and students are invited to come. There will be a meeting of the sewing club today at 3:05 in room 319."

Before I could continue reading the bulletin, a boy got up out of his chair and laid across a table, knocking books and paper to the floor. He just laid there, his whole body seemed to be jerking, as if he were having some kind of fit. The rest of the class just gazed at him silently.

"What's wrong with that boy?" I asked.

"He's high, that's all," a student answered.

"High off of what?" I asked.

"I don't know," the student answered.

I went toward the boy. Before I got to him, He jumped up, did a few back flips and shouted, "Oooo weeeeee!!!" And left my room.

The class broke out in laughter.

"Let's have the noise, let's have the noise." I told the class to settle down. Two students came in late. A boy and girl. As they walked in, the boy was gingerly feeling the girl on her behind. I shook my head. "Do you two have a late pass?" I asked.

"A what?" The boy mumbled.

"A late pass."

"No, we don't."

"Well, you'll have to go back and get one." The two students turned and left the room.

"Hey!" A boy yelled into the door.

"Keep your voice down," I said to a boy who wore a black baseball cap and green G.I. trench coat, "what do you want?"

"Come out into this hall. I want to bust your head open."

"You better go where you belong." I got up and went toward him.

before I got to the door, he took off running down the hall. I returned to the desk.

"Rinnnggg." The bell indicating the beginning of the first period. My homeroom left and made room for my first period class.

I passed the first period back their essays with the appropriate comments. Some students looked the essays over and put them in their notebooks, still others threw them in the trash or made paper airplanes out of them and sailed them across the room.

I decided to list 20 words on the blackboard and have the students look them up in the dictionary. I thought of the most difficult words, words like *conjugal* and *connubial*. I wanted to keep them busy.

It was funny I just happened to think of those particular words. I always told myself that I would never get married. The closest I got to marriage was staying with Karen, now that that was over, I was trying the bachelor life again and found it was less complicated but more lonely. I was

astonished that it seemed as if my whole first period class was looking up the words in their dictionaries. I figured it wouldn't last forever. Something had to go wrong.

Seeing that the class was unusually quiet, I took the time to write another poem. I had written 27 poems since December, 27 more and I'd have myself a book of poems. I scribbled a few stanzas and titled this poem,

'School Daze.'

17. School Daze

School daze, school daze,
When everyone breaks the rules days,
Cursing and fighting and ducking bricks,
Trying to teach lunatics.

Jimmy was my biggest problem child,
He came in class and just went wild.
I went to the Principal for help,
He told me to go home and eat some kelp.

School days, school days,
When everyone tries to act cool days,
Running and jumping and stopping fights,
Drinking and smoking and sleepless nights.

When I came in the room,
I heard something go 'boom!'
I looked at the desk,
And it was on someone's chest.

I walked out of school,
And they called me a fool.
When I turned around,
They called me a clown.
So I left, and never came back.

I finished the poem just as the second period bell clamored. The students passed their papers in. As my first period class filed out and my second period bopped in, I didn't notice anything out of place at first.

I noticed seven girls standing in front of their seats as I sat behind my desk. As if on signal, they all sat down simultaneously. Then I noticed just how little clothing they wore. As if by signal again, all seven of them crossed their legs in front of me. They all wore some of the shortest dresses I'd ever seen. They were trying to tease me. The more I looked, the more they tried to strike sexy poses.

"Surprise Mr. Johnson! I told you we would have a surprise for you today," one of the girls giggled as she pressed her hands along her shapely hips and dangled her right leg over her left. This was too much. As if sensing the struggle within me, they continued tempting me.

"Don't let them upset you Mr." A boy came to my rescue. "They're just trying to play with your mind." And they were doing a good job of it.

I looked away from the girls, and the tension drained momentarily. What made it so bad was that I hadn't had a woman in almost four months, and these young girls weren't helping my self-imposed abstinence any.

"Would you pass these papers out?" I asked a boy sitting a few rows down.

"Sure, I understand." The boy took the papers from me and passed them out. I was looking in every direction except the front.

"There are some words on the blackboard I want you people to look up in the dictionary. Turn in your papers at the end of the period." I said as the class grudgingly prepared to do the assignment.

The period was over before I knew it. Then the third period began. The second period went out, my third period came in. I sighed with relief that the girls were gone. I told myself that I would definitely have to watch out for female students that had surprises for me. I reminded myself to find a new girl friend. I instructed my third period to find the definitions of the words on the board once more.

"Mr. Johnson, are you Mrs. Johnson's husband?" A girl asked innocently.

"Who's Mrs. Johnson?"

"She's the Spanish teacher in 109."

"No, I don't know her."

"Mr. Johnson, Can I have a quarter so I can buy my lunch?" Another girl asked, unsure of my response. By now I was beginning to feel like the First National Bank, but I could not resist giving the students some chump change. I handed her the quarter and her face lit up.

"Thank you."

"You're welcome." I said as I mentally subtracted twenty-five cents from the change in my pocket. I had pretty well had my technique down pat for handling my classes. I tried to have something for them to do if the teacher didn't leave anything. If I couldn't find anything for them to do, I let them talk or do homework. Most of the time I tried to handle the situation myself if things got out of order. I contacted the office as little as possible because I didn't want the principal to be running to my class every five minutes. Administrators didn't care too much for subs that called the office too much.

"Why don't you be a regular teacher Mr. Johnson? I like your style," A student caught me by surprise. I thought about it for a moment. Even though I hated going to school and hated teachers when I was in school, I now gave the prospect some consideration. Being a regular teacher did have its advantages. I would make more money, be working full time and get several fringe benefits. Other teachers told me it was better being a regular. I would get to know my students and be in better position to discipline them. The students did have a tendency to take advantage of substitutes. I would call personnel later and find out the requirements.

"Mr. Johnson, you're a nice substitute." A student said.

"I am?" I said attempting to sound surprised.

"Yes, you are. Some of the teachers around here are so mean."

"The way some of you act, is enough to make anyone mean."

"Do you have any gum?" A student asked.

"Yes, I do, here." I just happened to have a few sticks with me.

"You punk!" I heard a boy yell at another boy on the other side of the room.

"Who are you calling a punk!?" The boy got up. I moved swiftly toward them hoping I could diffuse the situation.

"What's the problem," I said as I positioned myself between them.

"He called me punk. I'm not going to let him call me that and get away with it!" The boy yelled.

"Hold on now. I can't have you two fighting in here. If you two want to fight, wait until the bell rings and fight in the bathroom or something." The two boys eyed each other fiercely and suspended their hostilities. For the time being I had averted another confrontation.

"Rinnnggg," fourth period, my lunch period. After choking on a peanut butter and jelly sandwich, I decided to call personnel and see what courses I had to take in order to be a regular teacher. I went to the pay phone and dropped the coins in.

"Good afternoon, personnel," a pleasant female voice came over the phone.

"Yes, I'm a substitute teacher with a liberal arts bachelor's degree. Could you tell me what education courses I need to take to get a teaching certificate?" I asked.

"Hold on." There was a short pause, "let's see. You need a Bachelor's degree in your field and thirty more credits in education."

"Thank you, thank you very much." I hung up the receiver. That was quite a lot more courses I would have to take. I returned to my room and tried to envision myself as a regular teacher. The picture failed to materialize in my brain. Oh well, I wouldn't let that stop me. Just maybe, if I was determined, I could do it.

"Rinnnggg." Fifth period. I returned the papers to the class after they took their seats. I spoke to the class:

"The spelling and grammar of these essays was terrible. There were entirely too many run-on sentences. You have to watch your punctuation, capitalize at the beginning of a sentence and put a period at the end. A lot of you wrote less than a page. I wanted a whole page. If Ms. Corey had a chance to see these papers, she would be shocked. I know she's taught you how to write essays better than this." I finished criticizing the students, hoping that some of them would not make the same mistakes again.

"Give me my hat back Sammy," a boy said as two other boys were tossing his hat back and forth. This was ridiculous.

"You boys stop that and give him back his hat." I said to no avail. I headed toward them and tried to help the boy get back his hat. These boys were starting to irritate me. It was little foolish jokes like this that almost made me wish I was doing something else.

I felt like a perfect idiot as I tried to get the boy's hat back. As soon as I would run toward one boy, he would throw the hat to the other boy. Just as I got the two boys in a position where they could not throw the hat to each other without me getting it, they threw the hat around the classroom to the other students. I finally gave up in frustration. The students had tired of tossing the hat back and forth and gave the boy back his hat.

For the one thousandth time, I told myself I had to find another job. These kids were going to drive me up the wall. I had second thoughts about becoming a regular teacher.

The sixth period bell chimed. I awaited the final assault on my nervous system for the day. Despite the fact that my mind was clear and unclouded by any pills or wine, I was still becoming more tense day by day. I just dismissed it as some lingering after effects of coming off the wine and pills. If I could just make it until June. It was April now, just another month and a half and the school year would be over.

Then it hit me. A creeping feeling of desperation. A repressed feeling of wanting to walk out of school and not come back. A feeling of just giving up. I thought I had solved most of my problems when I had stopped drinking and taking pills. I had a bad feeling that my real problems were just beginning, and the bet with Matson was still on.

I gave the sixth period back their papers and told them that they could do better. But it seemed that my suggestions were falling on deaf ears.

"Can I have a pass?" A short, stocky muscular boy asked me in simulated anger.

"I'm not writing any passes for you to walk the halls," I said.

"I'm not going to walk the halls. I just want to go to the bathroom."

"Why didn't you go to the bathroom before you came here?" I asked. No answer, he then said again, "I want a pass."

I looked not at him, but through him, as if he wasn't there, trying to ignore him.

"I want a pass." The boy had not given up yet.

I looked at him and he looked at me. He was really starting to bug me.

"You're going to give me a pass or something!" The boy hollered and dropped his books on the floor and came toward me, as if he was going to try and make me give him a pass. I did not move, I just looked at him, hoping he would give me an excuse to tear his head off.

The boy stopped short of my desk and just stood there, feeling me out. When he saw that I did not get unraveled, he turned around and sat down. The seventh period bell dinged, fortunately my free period finally arrived. The students left and I gathered my things and left the building. The weather was warming up now and the day was clear and slightly windy. It was such a promising day, I decided to walk home. My apartment wasn't too far and I surmised that I could use the exercise.

As I walked down the street, I passed some of my students on the way. They recognized me and said, "Hi Mr. Johnson" or "Weren't you our substitute at school?"

And I would say "Hi" or "Yes I was," and keep walking.

Shortly, I saw a late model El Dorado Cadillac with gangster whitewalls pull up beside me. I thought it was Matson at first, but it turned out to be Leroy behind the wheel. It seemed like everyone had a nice ride besides me.

"Hey Cornell, can I rap to you for a minute?" Leroy muttered as he leaned forward in a semi-nod.

"Yeah, sure Leroy, what's up?" I said as I came closer to the car.

"Hop in, I'll give you a lift home while I run it down to you." "Run what down?" I asked as I got into the luxurious set of wheels.

Leroy eased down on the accelerator and the ponderous machine began to accelerate. He reached in his stash in the glove compartment and flipped the cap off of a doujie with one hand and held the wheel with the other. In a few seconds he sniffed the fine white powder and wiped his nose.

"Want a hit?" Leroy asked me as he turned the corner.

"No thanks," I said as I tried to impress him that I could resist the stuff. The last thing I needed was a hit of some doujie. I remembered how good it had been to me in the past. But that was in the past, I felt like a new person now and I was extremely cautious about putting anything in my body except food and water.

Leroy looked at me in consternation and then spoke: "I'm working for Matson now Cornell. He wanted me to offer you a proposition."

"A proposition? What kind of proposition?"

"Well, this is what it is. Matson figures it's no way you'll have more money than he will by September so in order to avoid a lot of hassle, he's willing to call the bet off if you'll work for him." Leroy croaked decisively.

I felt sick. "The bet isn't over yet, you can tell Matson that I'll be seeing him in September to collect my money," I boasted. "You can let me off here Leroy."

"Sure," Leroy said as he slowed the ponderous vehicle to a stop.

"See you later," I said and walked toward my apartment. Leroy pulled off without saying anything. I was glad he was gone. I knew Matson was serious about the offer, not because he thought he was going to loose the bet, but because if he won and I didn't have his money, he probably really didn't want to hurt me. But if it came to that, Matson knew he couldn't let me off that easily.

I got home and popped a T.V. dinner into the oven. I was getting fed up with junior high school assignments so I put in a request for a high school. It was difficult for me to get a high school, assignment. There were 47 junior high schools in the city and only 13 high schools. There were 169 elementary schools and 19 special schools. So the odds in getting a high school assignment were not too good.

Many substitutes tended to hold on to a particular high school assignment once they got one. I hoped that if I could get in on the high school level and stay there, my days might not be so rough. From what I'd heard about the high schools, it wasn't as stressful.

I gobbled down my T.V. dinner and looked at the news and the 'Tonight Show' before falling asleep. I dreamed again about Karen. I couldn't get her out of my dreams.

The phone rang and I received my first high school assignment. I got out of bed and fixed a quick breakfast and got to Lexington High School early.

Lexington was a brand new school. From the outside it looked more like a seven story modern office building than a high school, complete with football field, parking lot and surrealistic street lights.

I walked up the concrete ramp that led into a spacious foyer. I stood in the foyer and looked around. I had a choice of taking either an escalator or elevator up to the office on the second floor. I decided to take an escalator up. As the escalator eased me upward toward the second floor, I marveled at how well-dressed the students were. Everyone looked as if they were going to a party or something. My clothing was a poor comparison to the students' clothing.

I felt out of place among them. I had not seen so many well dressed young people in one spot before. I stepped off the escalator and walked into an executive looking office with carpet on the floor.

"I'm a substitute called in for Fanton," I said to a gray-haired woman behind the counter. She checked a notebook and said, "yes, you're in for Fanton." She handed me the sign-in sheet, "Sign here please." After I signed the sheet, she handed me the key. "This is to room 509, have a good day."

"Thank you," I said and left the office and got on an elevator.

I stepped off the elevator and unlocked the door. The room was so clean and neat and everything so new that I was almost afraid to touch anything, thinking I might contaminate it. My homeroom students flowed in. All of them looked like young adults, this was more like it, I told myself. I didn't have to lift a finger. A female student checked the roll for me and filled out the absentee slip and took it down to the office. I looked on the board and saw that the teacher had left work for all classes. I sat back and waited for the ringing of the first period bell.

After the bell sounded, I prepared myself for my first period. My first period came in quietly and took their seats. I indicated to the students what they were to do. Most of them immediately started working except for a few. The few who did not do the work, found something else to do quietly without causing any disruption to the rest of the class. I saw a young man raise his hand. This was the first time I had seen anyone raise their hand in quite a while.

"Yes?" I asked.

"I have a question Slim" the student asked. I had forgotten to put my name on the board.

"My name is Mr. Johnson."

"I'm sorry, Mr. Johnson. In number 3, do we have to write the equation for the roots of the quadratic equation or do we have to find the solution itself?"

I looked up at the instructions on the board that stated both had to be found. Algebra was one of my favorite subjects. "You have to find both," I said.

"Thanks," the student said and continued working.

"You sure you know what you are talking about?" Another student said.

"Of course I know, I've taken thirty something credits in math in college," I said.

"Of course he knows what he's talking about Kenny," another student came to my assistance. Of course I knew, I hadn't spent 4 years in school for nothing. Even though I had been out of school a few years.

My second period went by without difficulty and before I knew it, the third period, my free period, rolled around. I thought I would take a tour of the school. I walked down the well-lit halls to the gym. I looked in the gym and saw a large swimming pool. The students were taking turns practicing swan dives. This school had everything. Why couldn't the high school I had attended have been like this school? I continued on and came to the cafeteria which looked like a crowded restaurant. I returned to my room after stopping in a marijuana-smoke filled bathroom. It didn't bother me, I had walked into bathrooms like that before. It seemed like no matter where I went, I couldn't escape that smell.

My fourth period was uneventful and I took my lunch on the fifth period. The sixth period didn't show. I looked forward to the seventh period, my last period for the day.

I only had a handful of students come in to my seventh period. I routinely looked down the list of names on the roll and called out the names.

"George Jones," I said going down the list.

"Here."

"Freddy Bates."

"Here."

"Gloria Caldwell."

"Here."

'Patricia Jones."

It was now three o'clock pm. The students left the room. I remained at my desk. I felt lost, and alone. These past months I had been fooling myself, thinking I could go it alone without Karen. The bad dreams I had, I had tried to ignore but I was only deluding myself. I realized that I would not be able to make it without her. I knew I would have to find her somehow.

18. Where's Karen?

I took a few days off to look for Karen. I asked around the neighborhood during the day with no luck. At night I must have went to every club in town, but no Karen.

I decided to call every number in my phone book. I started in the 'A' section. I called Alphonso, Alice, Andrew and Amy, they didn't know anything. I started on the 'B' section and called Boo, Boe, Beverly, Bob, Bernice, Blackjack, Bamma-Jim, Bunky, Babba-Loo, Bruce and Bonnie, no good.

I was starting to tire and I still had twenty more sections to go. I thumbed to the 'C' section and dialed Candy, Cool-Aid, Chris, Cassie, Carol, Campbell. Confused was the last name on the list. I dialed his number after getting nowhere with the other numbers.

"Hallow."

"Hello, Confused?" I asked.

"Yah, who's this?"

"This is Cornell. Look here..."

"You got my five dollars?"

"I'll have it for you next week. That's not why I'm calling. I wanted..." Confused hung up before I could finish. I should have known better than to call him.

I turned to the 'D' pages and went down the line and called the Duke, Deborah, Donald, Daddy Roscoe, Dancer, Dorothy, Dandy, and Dick, to no avail.

I was thankful I only had one entry under the 'E' page, I called Egghead but got no answer. Most of the numbers I hadn't called in years and most of them were changed or disconnected. But I had to try everything. I turned to the 'F' list and dialed Francis and Fannie and Fatman and came up empty. I wiped the sweat from my brow and called the numbers in the 'G' section, Goofball, Gizzy, Gambling Man, Geechy, Goodboy, Goose, Goodstuff, Geraldine, Goochy. I scratched my head, who was Goochy?

I called the number anyway and found it was a wrong number. I looked and saw that Gail was the last name on the list. I dialed her number.

Five rings, six, rings, "come on Gail and answer the phone." I begged into the receiver.

"Hello."

"Hello, Gail?"

"Who's this?"

"Cornell."

"Oh Cornell, how are you?"

"Not so good," I said trying to sound more depressed than I really was. I had not seen Gail since the day she had knocked on my door. "I want to ask you something."

"Yes, Cornell?"

I swallowed and asked, "have you seen Karen lately?"

"No Cornell," she answered.

My chest became heavy and I started to say goodbye.

"But I did talk to her a few weeks later after that misunderstanding at the Purple Giraffe." Gail said.

"You did?" I became optimistic.

"Yes, Cornell. I told you I was going to talk to her and explain to her what happened. I ran into her down at the 'Bottoms Down' one night and we had a long talk."

"Did she believe you?"

"Yes, she did."

"Well why hasn't she tried to contact me?"

"She left me her address and said that if you really cared that you would come see her." Gail said.

I cursed myself for not letting Gail in that day.

"I came over your house one day but nobody answered the door. I thought you had moved or something." Gail explained.

"What's the address?" I asked.

"Wait, I'll get it."

I felt so foolish, I wished I had let Gail in that day. "Here, I have it. She lives at 1407 Shore way, Apartment 29."

"Thanks Gail, thanks a lot."

"Cornell?"

I wondered what she was going to say. "Yes?" I asked.

"Oh, nothing, goodbye." Gail responded.

I said bye and hung up the phone. I glanced at the clock, ten minutes to twelve. I was going over there tonight. I put my clothes on and left the apartment. I knocked briskly on the door, Karen please be home, I whispered to the door.

"Who is it?" That sounded like her.

"It's me, Cornell." It was pure torture wondering if she would let me in.

Karen released the chain and opened the door. She stood there in her bathrobe and head rag, but she still looked good to me. I grabbed and hugged her, kissing her intensely on the cheek at first, then in the mouth.

"Karen, I just talked to Gail. Why didn't you come back if you believed her?" I asked as I released her and she closed the door and put the chain back on.

"I had to be sure that you cared," she said as she looked at me and grinned.

I could deal with the dudes in the street and sometimes I could even understand the minds of the kids at school. But understanding women, especially Karen, continued to evade my understanding.

"Why didn't you call me up or something. I've been looking all over for you. I love you Karen, I care." The words came out unexpectedly to my surprise. Sometimes I had trouble showing my real feelings. I always tried to be mister cool.

"Gail said she went to give you my address but no one answered the door and she thought you had moved."

"I was going through some changes that day. I was home, but I didn't want to be bothered by anybody, I was going through cold turkey. Karen, I've stopped drinking and popping pills, I feel like a new person. I feel so much better." I said triumphantly.

"I'm glad you found me Cornell, and I'm happy you stopped drinking and getting high off those pills. I always knew you could kick the habit. Now we can really have some fun together without you getting all highed up."

I just looked at her and smiled.

"Are you still working?" She asked.

"Have you ever known me to be without a job?"

She laughed.

"No, don't answer that. Yeah, I'm still subbing." I said.

"Have you seen Matson?" Karen inquired.

"No, why?"

"Didn't Gail tell you?"

"Tell me what?"

Karen went over to the phone and picked up the receiver and began to dial.

"What are you doing?" I asked anxiously.

"I'm calling the police," Karen said.

"The police? For what?"

"On Matson. I'm going to tell them he's selling dope."

I grabbed the phone out of her hand and put it back on the hook. Karen gazed at me as if I were a madman.

"Why did you do that Cornell? I'm only trying to save you a lot of trouble. Gail was so concerned about you that she told me that Matson has already set aside ten thousand dollars to make sure he wins the bet and that if you didn't pay up when you loose, it would be too bad for you. Your only way out Cornell is to call the police and have him picked up for violation of his parole. That's what you're going to have to do Cornell, you can't possibly win the bet." Karen pleaded with me.

The odds had stacked themselves against me. It seemed as if Matson was obsessed with beating me and making me look foolish. I was determined not to give in just yet. I wasn't going to be intimidated by Matson's seemingly overwhelming advantage. But I couldn't bring myself to turn Matson in, I just couldn't.

What had started out as a friendly bet on money-making ability was quickly turning into a deadly contest of will and determination. What had happened to the odds? I thought Matson would be dead or in jail by now. But it seemed with every passing day the odds swung in his favor. I thought sure that Matson's habit would have eaten him up alive by now. I couldn't figure

out how a man with a habit could possibly hold on to ten thousand dollars for any length of time. Plus the fact that Matson was playing with the 'Big Boys' now I thought would increase his chances of going down.

    To the contrary, it looked like I would be the one to if not bite, at least maybe eat some dust. I hesitated and faltered for a solution to this brutal equation, but all I could see was a no win situation getting worse.

    "Don't turn him in Karen. If I play my cards right, I know I can win this thing." Was I living in a dream world?

    "There's something that's not adding up. When I find out what it is, I'll be home free." I was wishing and hoping.

    "All right Cornell, I hope you know what you're doing." Karen looked at me. For some reason she still seemed to have some confidence in me. I hope I wouldn't have to disappoint her.

    "Of course I know what I'm doing. Don't you know that they used to call me the genius?" I continued, "I didn't go to school four years for nothing Kay."

    I continued to convince myself and appease Karen's fears if not my own. Then I remembered that I hadn't so much as touched a woman since December. I pulled Karen toward me and hugged and kissed her like a maniac. It had been a long time. But now Karen and I were back together. Now I felt I could make it, as long as Karen was by my side.

19. Counter Attack

I felt on top of the world now that Karen was back. I valiantly knew I could deal better with situations since I had someone to talk to after a grueling day in school. Someone who cared about me, someone who would make the absurdities and inconsistencies around me worth enduring.

I felt that a part of me had been missing and was now back in it's proper place. How did I ever manage without her? The classroom fatigue the past months no longer seemed as bad. It was near the end of April when I came home worn out. I kept turning the situation over in my head about the ten thousand dollars Matson was supposed to have put aside. There was something that wasn't right. I felt the answer was right in front of my face, but I couldn't recognize it.

Karen looked at me and frowned, she knew I was worried. "Cornell, you're going about this all wrong. Why are you letting Matson make you do all the sweating? Why don't you make him sweat a little? For all we know, Matson could be bluffing about having ten thousand dollars set aside."

"I've thought about that, but how can I make him sweat?"

"Make him think you're doing better than you really are. Then maybe he'll get shaky and start to make some mistakes," Karen seemed to always have an answer.

That sounded like a good idea. I looked in the box where I kept my poems. It just might work.

"What are you doing Cornell?" Karen asked.

"If I could just get these poems published."

"That will take too long. And how do you know that the company you send it to will take it?"

"I'll send them to a vanity publisher where I have to pay. I'll ask them to send me a contract stating how much I have to pay. I'll take the contract and fix it up a little and make it look like they're offering me a straight royalty instead. Then I'll call Blackjack and Leroy over and tell them I just sold a book of poems for a fat sum. They'll go back and tell Matson and that should shake him up a little." I said.

"Now you are talking." Karen nodded in agreement.

"In the meantime I will have to get a hold of some school system letterheads and type a letter up saying I have been promoted to a regular teacher with retroactive pay going back to September and to be paid in a lump sum. I'll casually mention it to Leroy or Blackjack and show them the letter. Maybe Matson will get so worried he might want to call the bet off."

"I doubt if Matson will want to call it off." Karen said.

"It's worth a try." I sat down after pulling out my old typewriter and writing a few more poems to add to the collection. I titled the poems <u>School Daze</u> and looked through a magazine for the name of a subsidy publisher. Standard Press, that's where I would send them.

"How are you going to get the letterheads Cornell?" Karen asked while she folded some clothes.

"I'll get them from school tomorrow some way."

Reese Junior High wasn't anything to look at on the outside, and even less on the inside. I signed in at the office and observed the people behind the counter. There were two secretaries, one man and one woman who could either be the principal or assistant principal.

I glanced at my schedule as I entered the classroom. First period-duty, second, third period-classes, fourth period-lunch, fifth period-class, sixth period-free, and seventh period-class.

I survived the first two periods. Then my third period started.

After I took attendance, that's when the kids started acting up. One short boy in khaki brown pants was chasing another boy around the room, knocking desks and chairs over as they went.

"All right, sit down and you two stop running around this room like you're crazy or something." I called out to them.

They stopped and went back to their seats. I wondered if this was the way it would be all day.

"Don't worry Mr. Do you want me to keep this class straight?" A tall light-complexioned boy asked me confidently.

"Yeah if you think you can do it." And the boy did just that. He went around to each individual student that was showing off and got them in line with a few quick blows to the chest. After 30 minutes more of this madness, the bell sounded.

After breaking up five fights, ducking three erasers, two pencils, one trash can and hollering sixteen times for the students to get quiet, my lunch period finally arrived. I walked down to the office to try for some letterheads and pulled on the door, it was locked. Who ever heard of a school office being locked at lunch time, I asked myself.

I would have one chance left today to get what I wanted. I didn't think it would be this difficult.

My fifth period didn't show. The sixth period came, my free period and I walked to the office again. I walked in and the office was deserted.

That was strange. "Anybody here?" I asked as I looked into the adjoining offices for a sign of life, no one.

I decided to take advantage of the situation and rifled through the drawers. I pulled one drawer open and there they were. I scooped up a few letterheads and closed the drawer. I looked out the window and saw a crowd of people. I saw lights flashing as police cars and an ambulance pulled up. I went outside to see what was going on.

"What happened?" I asked one of the teachers standing around a boy stretched out on the ground.

"Someone tried to rob him and they shot him," the teacher said as paramedics came to the boy's assistance.

I felt a deep sense of frustration and anger. A student could not be on the school grounds without being assaulted and robbed and then shot. What was the school system coming too? The principal let the school out early and I returned to my apartment, at least I had the letterheads.

Karen greeted me with a kiss as I came through the door. I took my coat off and tossed the letterheads on the table. "How was your day?" She asked.

I didn't answer.

"What happened this time?"

"Someone tried to rob a boy on the school grounds and then they shot him," I said.

"That's terrible Cornell. What's wrong with those kids?"

"I don't know. I did get the letterheads. Let me type the letter up and get it over with. What do you think will be a good lump sum" Six thousand, seven thousand?" I asked as I put the paper in the typewriter.

"Seven thousand should be enough."

I typed up the letter and looked it over for errors. "Perfect, now I'll call Leroy, no, I better call Blackjack so it won't look so obvious. I'll leave the letter here on the table where he can see it. I know he'll go back and tell

Leroy and Leroy will tell Matson. The best defense is a good offense. Isn't that right Karen?"

"That's right," Karen agreed.

"It will be awkward to just ask Blackjack to come over. I'll have to buy a nickel bag from him to make it look good. You got five dollars?"

"Yes Cornell."

"Good." I said as I picked up the phone and dialed Blackjack. Blackjack answered the phone: "Hello."

"Hello Blackjack?"

"Yeah. What's up?"

"This is Cornell. Can I get a nickel bag from you?"

"I'm dead right now, the heat's on. I'll check around and see if I can run into some. Call me back in about an hour," Blackjack said and hung up.

The heat was on, I had not considered that happening. Maybe it might work out toward my advantage.

"Blackjack didn't have anything, he said the heat was on and for me to call back in an hour."

"The heat's on?" Karen looked at me.

"Yeah. That might be good. If the heat stays on long enough, it might cut into Matson's profits where he might have to use that so called ten thousand dollars to feed his habit."

"I doubt if it will affect him if he has a direct pipeline to the 'Big Boys' Cornell."

"I was just trying to look on the bright side."

An hour later I called Blackjack again.

"Blackjack? Could you get a hold of anything?" I asked.

"Yeah, I got it. The weight's not too good but it'll get you over," he said.

I didn't care how good it was, I just wanted to get him over to see the letter.

"All right." I responded.

"I'll be over in a few minutes," Blackjack said and hung up. "We're set Karen, he's on his way." I said and got everything ready.

Blackjack brought the nickel bag over and glanced at the letter. I pretended I didn't notice him. I told him if it was good I'd want some more in order not to make him suspicious. After he left I flushed the bag down the toilet and crossed my fingers.

20. Showdown With Matson

May went by almost too fast. I had received the contract from the subsidy company and they said it would cost me two thousand dollars to publish the poems. I fixed it up to look like they were advancing me five thousand and showed it to Leroy. Word spread in no time that I had become a 'big time' author.

The heat was still on and I couldn't have been happier. I'd gathered from the street that things were so dry that they were selling parsley flakes for marijuana and vitamin pills for goofballs. And the good dope was really hard to come by. The freeze so far had lasted about forty days. I calculated that if Matson had to use a minimum of hundred dollars a day from his stash, that would be four thousand dollars less from his ten thousand, if he still had that much, less another four thousand he would have to pay for minor expenses like bodyguards and other incidental items. I estimated that he would be lucky to have two thousand left.

I had heard that he was starting to take chances like selling bad stuff and fooling his parole officer. I marveled that he was still operating. I figured now was the time for me to make my move before it was too late.

I managed to secure a thousand dollar loan from the bank and Karen wrangled another thousand dollar loan from her credit union. I had somehow kept five hundred in my savings account and thirty-four in my checking. I knew I had to move soon, school was almost out and I knew I couldn't hold on to all the money for long and I doubted I could get more anytime soon. I didn't think I could fool Matson much longer about being a regular teacher or 'big time' author. It was the second week of June with a few more days of school left. I pawned the record player and T.V. and got two hundred dollars more which brought my total to two thousand, seven hundred and thirty-four dollars. I decided that now was the time to move the deadline up from September to two days from now.

"Karen, I think it is time to move the deadline up on the bet," I said after checking my cash. My day at school hadn't been bad, not bad at all.

"You're kind of pressing your luck aren't you Cornell?" She said as she folded her arms in dismay.

"I don't think we'll be able to hold on to this money for long. It's just a matter of time until Matson finds out about the letter and contract. The heat won't be on indefinitely. I better call the bet now. I know Matson's cash has got to be low. I want to get this bet over with, the pressure is getting to me." I said.

"You don't know for sure if Matson's cash is low or not."

"There's always one way to find out." I said.

"I don't know why you made the stupid bet in the first place. We're going through all this hell for what? A thousand stupid dollars! It's not even worth it." She continued complaining. "And if you loose, we'll be in debt even more. It just doesn't make sense."

"You know, you are right Karen, but the bet is already made. I have to deal with it now, the best way I know how. I'm tired of everything Karen. I'm tired of the maniacs at school. I'm tired of fooling Matson. I'm tired of borrowing money. I'm tired of worrying about the bet. I don't even care anymore if I win or loose, I just want to get it over with." I voiced all of my frustrations.

Karen didn't say anything for a moment. Then she spoke: "Do what you gotta do Cornell."

I picked up the phone and dialed Matson.

"Hello."

"Hello, Matson?" My voice was strained.

"Yeah."

"I have a proposition for you." I became more tense as I pushed for a showdown. I continued: "How about us moving up the deadline on the bet?" I didn't get a response from Matson.

"I was thinking of moving the deadline up to two days from now."

"I got a better idea," Matson elaborated briefly, "let's move the deadline up to tonight. I'll see you in about an hour." Matson finished and hung up before I could say a word. I was petrified. I wasn't prepared for this. Then I thought about it, two days might not make that much difference. But why was he in such a rush to get the bet over with?

"What did he say Cornell?" Karen asked me as I began to sporadically look out the window.

"He moved the deadline up to tonight and said he would be over in about an hour."

"I don't like it Cornell. Something's wrong, call him back and tell him you want to postpone the deadline." Karen urged me frantically.

I picked up the phone and called him again. I must have let the phone ring twenty times but no one answered.

"No answer Karen. What difference does it make. I will still have the same amount of money two days from now. Might as well go on and get it over with tonight," I said, full of uncertainty.

"Something's wrong Cornell, I can feel it. I don't like it, I don't like it at all. Matson had a reason for wanting to move the deadline up to tonight and I know it's got to be to his advantage," Karen said as she began to rub her arm nervously.

Before I could answer Karen, there was a knock at the door. Karen and I looked at each other and froze. I managed to gather my courage up to speak: "Who could that be? I hope it's not Matson so soon. Ten minutes haven't even gone by yet."

I walked toward the door cautiously and looked through the peephole, it was Leroy and Blackjack. I wondered what they wanted.

"It's Blackjack and Leroy, Karen. I didn't expect to see them tonight. They're probably coming back to see if I want another nickel bag or something that's all." I told Karen as I opened the door and let them in. Karen eyed them suspiciously and even I began to worry.

"What brings you two this way this time of night?" I asked them, trying to sound more natural and less agitated but it didn't work. Blackjack wore an all black outfit and black fur-collared leathered coat. Leroy dressed a little more conservatively in a ragged army camouflaged jacket and faded khaki pants.

"We came over to congratulate the new school teacher and 'big time' poet," Leroy growled with malice in his voice.

I looked toward Blackjack for some explanation but all I got back was an ice-cold stare. Apprehension was beginning to form in the air so thick that I could feel it start to close in on me.

"Yeah, I did manage to get a promotion to teacher and sell some of my poems." I wondered what game they were trying to run.

"Leroy," Karen spoke up boldly, "Cornell and I have something to do. We don't want to buy anymore nickel bags so will you two please leave."

Leroy looked at Blackjack and just snickered deviously.

"Look, I got things to do. What do you want Leroy?" I said nervously as I tried to calculate their intentions.

"We want your cash sucker!" Leroy screamed as he pulled out a thirty-eight from under his coat.

"What cash?" I made a foolish mistake by trying to play dumb. The next thing I felt was a stinging pain from the butt of the thirty-eight after Leroy bashed it against my head. I dropped to the floor and felt small trickles of blood drip down my forehead.

"Stop playing around! We know you got the money around here somewhere. I saw the contract and Blackjack saw the letter." Leroy yelled like a mad dog.

"Give it to him Cornell," Karen pleaded, "it's not worth getting shot over."

"I'm glad your lady talks with some sense," Blackjack grunted.

Resistance was futile. I struggled to my feet and reached behind the sofa, the barrel of Leroy's thirty-eight following every move I made. I came up with a brown box and handed it to Blackjack.

Blackjack flipped the box open and flicked through the bills and then nodded to Leroy. They backed slowly out the door after pulling the phone out the wall.

"Don't try to follow us unless you want some of this thirty-eight!" Leroy yelled as he eased out the door. I heard the frantic clatter of their feet down the steps, a car starting and then tires screeching.

Now I realized that the letter and contract were mistakes. They worked too well, so well that I'd convinced Leroy and Blackjack that I had made a lot of money. I had set my own self up. Instead of the letter and contract helping me win the bet. They had become the very things that had caused me to loose the bet. I knew it was over now. If Matson just walked in the door with a penny, he would win. And where would I get the $1,000 to pay him off? I began to shiver in anger and defeat. Karen's sad eyes met mine, and I knew we were both thinking the same thing.

"You gotta get out of here Cornell! You better run! Before Matson gets here, you have to get out of town. I'll go next door and call the police on Leroy and I'll stall Matson as long as I can when he gets here. Get out of here now Cornell, hurry!"

I grabbed my coat and checkbook. I climbed out the back window and dropped to the ground, I wasn't taking any chances. I was frightened to the point of recklessness. I wrote a bad check for some traveling money, at the store on the opposite side of my apartment complex. I looked around as I walked swiftly down the street.

I jumped in a cab and headed for the bus station. At least I might have a jump on him if he was heading for my house. I wondered if Matson had sent Blackjack and Leroy to rob me? That way he could make sure he would win the bet. Would I ever find out? I didn't have time to think about that now.

I looked out into the stars-speckled night sky as the cab sped me to my destination. It seemed as if all I had tried to accomplish had gone down the drain because of a foolish bet. I had spent 4 years in college, instead of getting smarter, I had gotten dumber.

The cab pulled up in front of the bus station. I paid the cabbie and ran toward the ticket window. I got a one-way ticket to Pittsburgh. Matson would never think of looking for me there. I went over to the soda machine, looking back over my shoulder all the way. I dropped a quarter in and pulled the soda out the slot and turned around and saw Matson coming through the door!

How had he found me so fast? It's all over now, I grimaced. The stories people told about their whole life passing before them when they thought they were going to die seemed to be coming true for me too. I couldn't believe how fast my thoughts were flashing in those few seconds as Matson came closer and closer. All through my life I was just the type of person that didn't mean anyone any harm. I was just trying to survive. Why me, I asked myself? I never really hurt or killed anybody. Why couldn't I get my life together? There must be an answer to this madness somewhere.

The fear almost turned my legs to stone. For the first time since I had gone to Sunday school I spoke a prayer. I hoped there was a God listening to my prayer, wherever he may be.

"God, if you're listening, please help me." I began to remember what the people from that church had tried to tell me about God. Could they be right? Did Jesus really care about us? Could he help me in my desperate situation? Somehow movement returned to my legs.

I ducked back behind the soda machine and watched Matson. I couldn't believe what I saw. He went to the ticket window and bought a ticket. He then walked quickly to the boarding gate. He kept looking back over his shoulders. Matson boarded a bus, the doors closed and the bus left the station. I couldn't figure out what was happening.

I ran to a phone booth and with trembling fingers dialed next door to my apartment. The man next door answered and I asked him if Karen was still there, he said she was and put her on the phone.

"Karen, I just saw the strangest thing." I said trying to maintain my composure.

"Cornell, are you all right? I called the police."

I interrupted her. "I just saw Matson get on a bus and it left the station." I stuttered.

"That's what I thought he'd do. I told the police about Leroy and Blackjack robbing us and they're after them now. I also told them about Matson selling dope but they told me they didn't have to worry about him. The word was out that he had messed up the 'Big Boys' money while the heat was on by using more than he could sell and now there's a contract out on him." Karen explained.

"Are you still there Cornell?" Karen asked.

"I love you Karen. And you won't have to worry about me making anymore stupid bets. I think my betting days are over." I said triumphantly. I started to relax, something I hadn't been able to do for a long time. In a way, I felt sorry for Matson. We had grown up together. Sometimes I wondered if

Matson even cared about that anymore. Still I hated to see him go out like this. But I was grateful, not because Matson had a contract out on him, but that it seemed God had answered my prayer. I would not have to worry about the stupid bet anymore.

"Karen, let's get married, and let's start going to church."

"Get married? Go to church?" Karen couldn't believe my words.
"You know Karen."

"Yes Cornell."

"I love you Karen. And there is a God after all, and I think his son's name is Jesus!"

21. Letter of Gratitude

Democracy City Public Schools
Division of Personnel
Landmark Building

219 18th St. City
June 20, 1974

Mr. Cornell Johnson
267 21st St., N.E.
Democracy City

Dear Substitute Teacher:

We take this opportunity to thank you for your services as a substitute teacher for the education and welfare of the youth of our city during the school year 1973-1974.

Again, we thank you for your sacrifices.

Sincerely yours
Wilhelmina Patterson
Director

WP ;kvr

THE END